DORIAN GRAY VERSUS VERSUS REANIMATOR

PETE RAWLIK

CHRISTOFER NIGRO

KEVIN HEIM

COVER ART: JIM FAUSTINO OF LUNGGA CREATIVES

TITLE LOGO DESIGN: ELDEN ARDIENTE OF LUNGGA CREATIVES

DEDICATIONS

To my kids Elena and Tessa. – Pete Rawlik

To the memory of my beloved grandparents, Thomas and Trudie Nigro; to the memory of the father I never knew; and to the strength and inspiration provided to me by the Gods of Asgard... Merry Meet to Odin, Thor, Freya, Freyr, Idunn, Balder, Tyr, Loki, Hermod and the rest of the Ancient Ones. – Christofer Nigro

Like all my fiction, this story is dedicated to Helen Edgar and Scott Dempley, who helped me turn fan fiction into fan fact. And I guess my mom and my kids are important, too. – Kevin Heim

TABLE OF CONTENTS

A VIEW OF THE TRENCHES

Pete Rawlik

November 1916

I am not fond of telling tales about my life; even the task of documenting my experiments I leave to the skilled hand of my partner and near-constant companion. Still, there are times when the two of us were separated and consequently there are experiences and adventures of which he knows almost nothing. This was the case in November of Nineteen Hundred and Sixteen when he was attending to the wounded in Albert, and I was closer to the front in what was left of the village of Morval.

Weeks earlier, the village had been held by the enemy, and in the process of taking the French town from the Germans, the British had done their best to turn it into rubble and ruin. Even the venerable church of St. Vaast had been leveled. Now, well behind the line, it held little strategic value save as on the road between the front and command. It was here in a ramshackle barn that my field surgery was established. Here the wounded were brought to me to be treated as best I could before being sent back to the trenches or hauled away to be sent home.

It was also here that I assessed the bodies of the dead for possible use in my experiments. It had been about a year since the loss of my colleague Clapham-Lee and the debacle that followed. I was keen not to repeat the errors I had made there. Hence, I confined my studies to those bodies that were

1

more or less intact, particularly avoiding those who had suffered through decapitation. It was in my review of the bodies of the recently deceased that I came across a particularly eligible corpse.

Most of the bodies that I reviewed suffered from devastating wounds inflicted by German Spandau MG 08s, inferior copies of the Vickers guns used by the British forces. Despite their inferiority, the MG 08s still were capable of wreaking significant physical damage on the body, which left the corpse unfit for my needs.

Thus, when I found a casualty completely intact without any sign of significant damage, I was rather pleased. My first thought was that perhaps Lieutenant D. Gray had been the victim of a concussive blast of some sort, for his uniform was in tatters, but his body was, save for a few bruises, nearly injury free. He was a magnificent specimen, tall and well built, of good Anglo-Saxon stock. His eyes were blue, his hands were meticulously manicured, and his fine dark hair well groomed – near impossibilities in the trenches.

The other thing I found odd was the state of his skin. I examined the man from head to toe, and what I found, or more importantly didn't find, were scars or blemishes of any sort anywhere on his body. One would have thought that the man had been exposed to some disease or another, or at least cut himself on a knife, or banged a knee. But there was nothing, save for the recent bruising. He was as clean as a newborn babe and by my determination a prime candidate for undergoing my reanimation treatment.

It was easy to steal the body. People, and especially soldiers, tend to avoid the places of the dead, the morgue in particular. All I had to do was borrow the wheelbarrow used to move bodies from the surgery to the morgue and utilize it in reverse. The surgery was empty, and a perfect place to carry out my experiment. The fighting had been in a lull for a few days and so the area was devoid of patients. It was, however, a condition that could change at any minute, so I took a moment to run to the hill and look down the road. I could see for miles; it was one of the reasons the Hun had been so keen to hold the position, and why they had held it for so long.

The road was clear, I had all the time that I needed. I was back in the makeshift surgery within minutes, only to find myself facing the strangest of situations. The surgery was empty, the body of my intended experiment – Lieutenant D. Gray – had vanished, leaving the tattered remnants of his uniform behind!

I reached for my instrument tray, to hide it I suppose, but the key instrument – the syringe containing my reagent – was no longer there. I panicked and scanned the room for it. Imagine my surprise when I heard a voice from one of the far corners.

"Looking for this?" It was the lieutenant in a state of partial dress, and he was waving my reagent syringe about. "It isn't a gun or a knife, but why do I feel that this little contraption and what it contains would be considered just as dangerous?"

I walked toward him. "Yes, used without skill it can be quite devastating, whereas in the proper hands the results can be... invigorating."

"I'm sure," he said while placing the syringe in my hand, "and you were going to use this on me?"

"You were dead."

"And now I am not."

"Yes," I murmured, securing the syringe containing my invaluable formulation. "This is an occurrence that I have some experience with, albeit usually following the administration of my medical expertise. Your spontaneous revitalization is quite unprecedented, Lieutenant Gray."

"Would you like me to explain?" He smiled and continued buttoning up a shirt he had lifted from a shelf

3

where we stored excess clothing gathered from the deceased. "And do call me Dorian."

"Nothing would please me more, Dorian."

"Can't – I haven't a clue." He chuckled a bit. "Some sort of magick, I suspect. There is a painting involved, a portrait I had commissioned by a rather talented artist who was quite devoted to me. He never revealed what he did, or how he did it. But here I am nonetheless."

"And this painting, it keeps you from being injured? But you *were* dead, so there is some consequence. What is the delay? Is it constant, or proportional to the damage inflicted?"

Dorian smiled and rubbed his chin. "That, my friend, would be telling, although it might be interesting to experiment and discuss your opinion of the results, Doctor - I'm sorry, I didn't catch your name."

"West, Herbert West, of Arkham, Massachusetts."

"An American, attached to the Canadians, I see. Did you come out of patriotism, or for some other reason?"

I scoffed. "My motivations are my own business."

"Not a patriot, then," he almost sneered. "Patriots are always more than willing to inform you of their noble intentions."

"And you, Lieutenant Dorian Gray, are your motivations patriotic in origin?"

He sat down to put on a pair of boots. "They may have been once, at least in part. One does what one can for King and Country, but…"

"As long as it doesn't interfere with your own schemes." He gestured at me politely. "You are a rather intelligent schemer, aren't you?"

"One does one's best. So, may I assume you are here in Morval because of the church of St. Vaast?"

At this suggestion, I was admittedly puzzled. "I go where Command sends me, more or less. I am a man of medicine,

4

a scientist. My work is rather dependent on a steady supply of the dead. I've no interest in churches or their saints."

"You should have an interest in this one. Vaast, known as Foster in Britain and Gaston in France, was from the coast. My research suggests Cherbourg, but he is more venerated here in the eastern provinces and the lowlands. He was an advisor to Clovis, the King of the Franks, and it was Clovis bearing witness to Vaast's miracles that converted him to Christianity."

"And what were these so-called miracles?"

Dorian giggled. "The usual stuff: healing the lame and the blind, filling empty wine casks, and of course, raising the dead using a luminous green vapor." He saw my eyes grow wide. "I thought that would pique your interest; it was just one of many references that I intend to research."

"There are others?"

"Of course. I'm sure you've heard of Frankenstein and Dracula, but there is also a sect of blind monks in Spain, and there are rumors of a ghost 'haunting' the Opéra Garnier in Paris, and of a lich in Prague. Then there are the stories of the man that has gained power over the royal family in Russia, the 'Mad Monk' Rasputin; they say that he is like me, that he cannot be killed. I would investigate such tales and determine their veracity or falsehood."

"And what do you expect to find here in Morval?"

"Vaast's relics were housed in an abbey named for him in the city of Arras, just a little north of here. At the outbreak of the war, it was thought best that the bones be removed for safe keeping, and some were sent here to the church in Morval. Intelligence suggests that the Huns looted the church before they were forced to retreat. My sources suggest that they've consolidated their plunder in the village of Le Transloy."

DORIAN GRAY VS. REANIMATOR
A View of the Trenches
Pete Rawlik

I thought back to the maps I had seen hanging in the command shed. "That's about two miles behind enemy lines."

"Yes."

"You'll be shot."

"Probably multiple times. That is actually the plan."

"To be shot? It will never work."

"Of course, it will. I can be shot multiple times and still make progress. After that, I fall down dead, for just a little while. I wait for the Huns to move on as I heal, and then get up and make some more progress. Then I find what I'm looking for and work my way back. Returning from there is the easy part. I know for a fact that there is going to be a major offensive two days from now. If I have any luck the Allies will just roll over me and I'll wake up back here in your morgue."

"You're mad," I told him outright.

He shook his head. "I'm not mad, I'm British… and I'm rather invulnerable." He could see that I was having a difficult time accepting what he was proposing. "Trust me, Herbert, I've done this before."

I led him outside and we went to where the hill gave a good view of the front lines. We could clearly see the warren of trenches that the Allies had built into the landscape, and the counterpart that had been constructed by our enemy just yards away. It was as if some mad titan had taken a weapon and laid the earth itself open, leaving behind a bloody and ragged scar which men scavenged about like vermin.

On both sides, we could see the crude sandbag towers that held both snipers and machine guns, and between these the deadly razor wire that one side or the other had deployed. It was perhaps the deadliest place on Earth, and my new acquaintance wanted to trek over it, scramble through the opposite trench, and then cross miles of enemy territory, just so that he could retrieve the bones of some saint that I had never heard of.

"You really think that you can make your way through that and then back again intact?"

"There and back again? No problem. Intact? Well, that depends on your definition, and how much help you're going to be."

"How exactly can I help?" I asked, fearful of what the response might be.

"You've seemed to collect quite a bit of clothing and equipment from your fallen comrades. Not to mention, by your own admittance… the remains of your fallen comrades themselves. Where exactly do you keep the things you loot from the bodies of the dead?"

It was only then that I realized that he was very clever, and that his plan might have a possibility of succeeding.

END

ATTACK OF THE DEAD MEN

Christofer Nigro

Dorian Gray's Journal, My Time in the Trenches, November 1916

"So that I understand this correctly, Lieutenant Dorian Gray," West said to me with a knowing scowl of trepidation, "you want me to utilize my reagent to… revive several of these German soldiers and send them to accompany you through the trenches?"

I smiled. "Congratulations on hearing me correctly the first time, mate. I plan on getting shot often enough while *en route* to Le Translov. We may as well put these chaps to use drawing some of the fire from me and serving as distractions. They are not exactly doing much good laying on the slabs rotting away or serving as a banquet for fly larvae, are they?"

"They are serving a purpose well beyond that, Dorian. They are the raw material for my experiments; in utilizing the chemical and medical sciences to do nothing less than conquer death itself. Most of us mere mortals do not have the good fortune of having an image of ourselves on canvas to absorb our fatalities."

It was then that I realized working with the good Dr. Herbert West was not going to be as easy as that. He was a most difficult man, and if I am to be completely frank with myself in my own memoirs, I must confess that he could be unsettling and intimidating in a manner that few others I have had the displeasure of meeting could match.

DORIAN GRAY VS. REANIMATOR
Attack of the Dead Men
Christofer Nigro

Like the portrait that my dearly departed Basil Hallward created for me, Herbert has found a means of potentially eliminating human death. Unlike my painting, however, the good doctor's chemical – alchemical? – method can be made available to the masses rather than a rare personal heirloom. I would wager, however, that it also makes far more of a mess than one of Basil's paintings.

"Allow me to remind you, my newest friend, that in a world like this, particularly one that can produce wars such as the one we are now in the midst of, you are not likely to find dead bodies in short supply. And if such a scarcity were to present itself, I do get the impression that you may not be above taking a life to keep your slabs occupied and your work going."

The resultant expression on Herbert's face was one that I did not care to look upon again. So, I do believe I had made my point.

"I would think… I can loan you some of my raw material here for the purpose you ask. Procuring those items of St. Vaast can prove an extraordinary boon to the work I do and would be most useful in the hands of those few like us who seek to unlock the secrets of immortality. The gods of this universe must cease being stingy with sharing that gift, and if I must take the role of Prometheus himself in granting this blessing to humanity, then so be it."

Again I smiled, hoping to make it look as affable as possible. "Good man! There is much for us to gain here, and you can provide me with the company I need during my trek over the trenches."

"I must warn you, however," Herbert began as he filled a syringe with his iridescent green liquid, "the current iteration of my reagent is… not without its flaws. Once injected, the dead will rise, but they will no longer have the minds of sane, rational men. They will behave… well, psychotically, to be blunt. And they often attack the living on sight with maniacal

9

fury, quick to make them into cadavers as well... albeit of the sort that does not walk."

"That sounds most splendid! For war needs violent men to fight it, and those who behave like your revivals will be quite the useful tool on the battlefield."

"You do not fully understand me, Dorian. It means that they will not exactly follow your orders. I have had some success with performing lobotomies of a sort that has made them more compliant to my direction under certain circumstances, but this is not an ideal time or location to perform such a procedure. They may very well cause you the same sort of... inconvenience as the armed members of the *Deutsches Heer* out there. Their cognizance does not function on a level where they distinguish friend from foe."

"I have taken that into full consideration, my good doctor. They need not follow any direction other than the literal path in which I will be running. Once they are out in the trenches and they see kraut soldiers out and about, I gather they will do what is required of them sans any need for explicit orders. Or, they shall get blasted to pieces in the attempt, which will serve to draw enemy fire from me. And speaking of armed men..."

I pointed towards a door leading to the second, much smaller room of the ramshackle hut that Herbert was forced to work within, knowing what such spaces were often used for out here. "May I surmise that you have armaments stored in there that these men once used to dispense death to the Allies? I doubt any good German soldier entered this battlefield without them."

"You would be correct. I have a few confiscated rifles in storage."

Herbert walked over to a metal door separating the main lab in the cabin from a much smaller room that was hardly larger than a closet. He opened the bolt-locked entry, and I beamed in delight at the cache of goods I saw sequestered

10

within. As a man of science who utilized chemicals to work his deviltry, the doctor hadn't much use for such items... save perhaps as an occasional means to acquire some needed material for his experiments.

His tools of choice were the syringe and the scalpel; for me, a good sword in hand would often do, but for a battlefield such as this, the Gewehr 98 I saw looked as lovely to me as a cheap whore in a Brussels bordello. The removable bayonet attached to its fine wooden underside made the piece look lovelier still.

"This will do quite nicely."

I procured the rifle, pulled back its bolt, and picked up a stripper clip with a most impressive set of 7.92×57mm Mauser ammo for easy reloading.

"I am now off to the trenches to attend church, so to speak. In the meantime, Herbert – may I call you that? – please do find some of the bodies that are most intact and perform your chemical wonderment upon them. An 'Attack of the Dead Men' is about to commence that will make Osowiec Fortress look like a pleasant social gala by comparison."

***

I boldly ran into the kraut-held trenches, my purloined Feldgrau tunic proudly showing off the colors of the German Empire. That was doubtlessly confusing to the soldiers who stepped out of the man-made furrows in the ground to see what the strange straggler was all about. However, that initial level of bewilderment was naught compared to that caused by the maniacal howls of Herbert's horde of reanimates that followed close on my heels in an attempt to run me down. I heard several shouts and curses in the German language as several canisters were hurled in the direction of myself and the loud, freakish cavalcade following closely on my heels.

Damn it all to Hell! The white star on those containers indicate they are filled with some combination of chlorine and bromide. This will not *be pleasant.*

A light hissing sound was heard as the ominous cloud of greenish-yellow gas began spewing out to engulf the field in front of me. Thankfully, my dearest James was not present to confront this threat.

I was equally thankful that the reanimates were mindless enough to rush right into the choking mists rather than retreat in the opposite direction, as would living soldiers upon seeing the very visible cloud. All that the still-living krauts would see were several figures following me into the gas and they raised their rifles in preparation to fire. The uniforms on the running dead were tattered enough that they were hardly identifiable in the dark as German military raiment.

I began coughing and gagging as the noxious mist assaulted my eyes, nose, and mucous membranes. I fell to the muddy ground below me and patiently waited for these effects to pass. I could merely wonder how damage to the esophagus and lungs could manifest in any visible fashion on the portrait that holds the secret to my immortality, but the eyes on the painting must now appear swollen and red.

The soldiers saw me land on my knees and crawl out of the gas cloud. After acquiring the nerve to approach me, since the scorching haze was several feet behind, they were about to receive a bloody cruel surprise – and I do mean *bloody.*

Two of the reanimates emerged from the cloud, the chlorine mists having concealed their presence. Never did these kraut wankers expect any seeming men to remain standing in such a thickly concentrated cloud of gas, let alone running. If the lungs of these ambulant dead men could be scorched by this substance, they showed no sign of being disabled from it. Their eyes were red and swollen as one would expect from such exposure, but this seemed to only increase their characteristic rage.

Herbert did not exaggerate when he told me the state of mind such reanimated blokes would be in after his devilish chemicals had brought them back from beyond. Clearly, not all of them had returned from that unknown frontier, however; their cognizance seemed to have remained wherever it goes upon one's mortal demise.

"Mein Gott!" were the only words the first soldier could utter as a howling dead man rushed out of the billowy cloud and charged at him.

So startled was he that his nose was bitten clear off his face by the running reanimate before he could raise a rifle in defense. One of his fellows released a salvo of lead on the bloodthirsty cadaver with a semi-automatic rifle likely purloined from the French military, shredding the creature's re-activated flesh to pieces.

The second soldier then met his demise as I opened fire on him, the high-caliber bullet taking his lower jaw clear off his face. Two other soldiers began rushing in my direction and I felt a sharp pain as I took a bullet in my left shoulder. Before they could release a fusillade on me, however, three more reanimates ran out of the cloud and descended on them.

This pair of krauts managed to shred the first of the attacking dead trio to bits of chemically revived flesh with their respective semi-automatic fire but the remaining two were upon them a moment later. The maniacal fervor with which Herbert's reanimates move when seeking to harm a still-living man was nothing less than astounding to behold. These soldiers were strong men, but the adrenalin-fueled insanity of these unliving lunatics swiftly bit, kicked, and pummeled the Teutonic warriors into bleeding heaps.

These two reanimates then rose up and turned their wild-eyed gaze upon me, the blood of their victims soaking their tattered uniforms and smearing their mouths. Could they even see me clearly after the bad number that gas had done on their eyes? I quickly realized the threat they presented to me in addition to the kraut fighters. I raised my own rifle in my defense only to be knocked to the ground by three rounds of lead blasted into my sternum, stomach, and throat by another attacking soldier of the living German variety.

Now that... hurt.

Clearly believing I had been killed, the duo reanimates ran by my fallen form towards the standing infantryman. He swore at the charging fiends with colorful kraut obscenities as he opened fire in his retort. One of them had the top of his skull blown off but the other slammed into the soldier just after his cohort in carnage had fallen, the force of the charge knocking the kraut to the mud-soaked ground. As my consciousness began to fade, I beheld a blurry vision of the moving dead man taking the soldier's rifle and using its solid steel butt plate to smash his face into wads of bloody meat with repeated, frenzied blows.

I felt nervous as I faded out, worried as to what the remaining animate corpse might do to my form during its brief period of healing stasis. Would he smash my face in with the pilfered rifle as well? Then again, what would be the point of that if the wanker thought I was deader than he was? They did seem to prefer thrashing the living, not dead men who truly acted the part.

Might the bloody bastard attempt to bugger me while I slept? That was an act I preferred to receive (or give) while conscious, mind you, and despite my notorious debauched tastes not even I relished the idea of a dead maniac puncturing my back doorway (would a vampire count, however? A question to ponder elsewhere in my journal). Needless to say, my state of mind was not a good one as darkness briefly overwhelmed me.

DORIAN GRAY VS. REANIMATOR
Attack of the Dead Men
Christofer Nigro

***

What actually occurred during the minutes or hours – one loses track of time in such instances – of my stasis appears to have been different than what my overactive imagination had pondered.

I awakened, as I always did, to no sign of injuries or pain whatsoever; my portrait, safely hidden back in England, had taken all the damage for me as it always did. Only holes in my tunic displayed any evidence that a volley of bullets had hit me in vital spots. I stood up only to find myself staring at a shadowy figure standing several feet away from me, partially concealed by a fog composed of a mixture of soot and chlorine gas.

It was just my luck that this turned out to be the remaining reanimate of that group. Like a lunatic, it continued staring at me for endless seconds with the inhuman patience of the unliving. Something about that bastard made him uncertain but apparently willing to stick around as long as it took to find out if I had truly passed beyond the veil.

No sooner had I gotten up healed of all injury than the damnable dead chap howled like a man truly depraved and ran at me with clear intent to do to me what he had already done to that kraut soldier. I reached to the ground for my rifle with due haste, but before I could bring it to bear the walking cadaver was on top of me.

I tried holding the damned thing back, but it bit into my right ear and tore off the fleshy lobe in its teeth. I screamed in pain and swore at the blighter. Then I elbowed the wanker in the face as hard as I could, causing it to move back an inch with twin streams of dark-colored blood flowing out of its flaring nostrils.

For the record, its face still looked human but was terribly wild-eyed with a truly unkempt mop of hair atop the head, as if it was an escapee from an asylum. Its eyes were glassy and gray, though also swollen with reddened whites and irises due to continual exposure to the chlorine-bromide gas mixture. The infernal thing quickly recovered from my blow and howled in greater anger than before. Then the ghoulish wanker resumed its attack, which I managed to block by holding my rifle between us like a staff. The relentless reanimate pounded and struck at my weapon like a madman, finally knocking it out of my grasp.

I dropped to the ground to recover it, but the vile thing placed its thick-booted foot on the gun's barrel, holding it down. Swiftly detaching the bayonet, I thrust it clear into my attacker's gut. The walking dead man bellowed in seeming pain and moved back a few steps. Then it looked down at its perforated bowel area more in confusion than anything else. The damnable beast did not go down, however; instead, its arms reached out to me, and it screamed in anger as blood mixed with salivary foam poured out its gaping mouth.

Following that, it proceeded to attack a third time. I shouted at my attacker while slicing off all ten fingers of its outstretched hands with a single wicked swipe of my blade.

"You need to stay down, sir! Only *I* may walk again on this battlefield after dying!"

With that proclamation, I sliced the bastard's throat. The thing's fingerless hands instinctively tried in vain to block the blood flowing out of its neck wound as it gargled and stumbled about. It was then easy enough to sever its head with a final swing of the bayonet.

These damned bastards are equal parts impedimentary and useful to my trek towards Vaast's church, I mused to myself as I recovered my rifle and reattached the bayonet to its underside. *Speaking of which...*

I touched my wounded ear to see that the lobe had fully grown back. Next, I gazed about the field of trenches to get my bearings as best I could. The effects of the gas were likewise nullified thanks to my "gift" so that my eyes were no longer subject to painful swelling and obscured vision. It seemed I had managed to run almost a mile and a half towards my two-mile goal, now being in the outskirts of Morval and about another twenty minutes of running distance from Le Translov.

It was then that I heard the sounds of shouting in Deutsch accompanied by gunshots and numerous howls of fury that I could easily recognize coming from at least a dozen more reanimates in the midst of both giving and receiving bloody mayhem. How many of those cursed things did my new doctor friend inject with that wonder fluid of his? There certainly seemed to be many corpses piled up in that bunker, which was no surprise considering the use of those new heavy Browning machine guns Her Majesty's infantrymen brought to bear against the krauts over the past week.

But did Herbert have to send so many of them? Was he enjoying this whole soiree a bit more than was necessary to provide me with the diversion I needed?

It was obvious from the sounds of carnage that the number of German soldiers was greatly exceeded by the doctor's walking dead men less than a quarter mile to the east. So, while many of the dead men would be reduced to unmoving cadavers again, that entire ensemble of krauts would be in pieces within minutes. After that, the reanimates left standing would start in my direction again, doubtless by following my trail across the muddy ground.

I thus resumed my race towards the ersatz Church of St. Vaast in the village of Le Translov, determined to reach it before the animated cadavers reached me. Of course, my rifle was at the ready at every moment; I just hoped it would be enough to secure my timely arrival.

DORIAN GRAY VS. REANIMATOR
Attack of the Dead Men
Christofer Nigro

***

No sooner had I entered the boundary into Le Translov than a bullet hit me in the right leg. I stumbled to the ground, doing my best to ignore the pain. A kraut was about, and I forced myself to hold my rifle while looking around for the damned sniper.

Another shot was fired and this time the bullet missed, but just barely. I turned and fired in the southeastern direction from my position since that was where the gunshot had originated. This move was followed by silence, so I had no idea if I had hit the sniper or not. I then just barely heard the sound of booted footsteps sloshing towards me through the mud in the opposite direction before a different soldier emerged from the darkness. I turned and released a shot, striking him in the throat. A stream of blood spewed from the puncture wound in his Adam's apple as the man fell to the ground, more future raw material for my friend Dr. Herbert West.

Then another bullet came from the southeast and struck me in the arm. I swore loudly and dropped my rifle. The soldier stepped out from the shadows with his Mauser pointed directly at my face. His own countenance was a mask of rage, determined to do me in for the glory of the Central Empires.

"Bloody hell," I whispered aloud, prepared to be sent into another stasis mode just when I was almost within spitting distance of the church.

"Mach dich bereit zu sterben, britischer Hund!" was what he shouted as he pulled back the bolt of his Mauser and prepared to inundate me with lead.

That was when I saw three more figures run to his side from out of the shadows. Only these were not reinforcements – they were another trio of reanimates who had gotten through the battle with this kraut's mates-in-arms further back. He turned towards his strange attackers and began emptying his clip into the lot of them. The first in line had its guts blown out its belly and the thing fell on top of its steaming bowels without moving again. Dead wanker number two was hit in the sternum but kept on charging while screaming like a banshee in heat, ignoring the bullet embedded in its breastbone.

These remaining two reanimates pushed the soldier to the muddy ground, causing him to lose his rifle in the process. The injured one slumped on top of the screaming fighter and bit two of his fingers off; whereas the second lifted the gun and smashed the screaming fopdoodle's face into a pulp of gnarled bits with several vicious blows. This ghastly duo did my work for me in admirable fashion, giving my bullet wounds the seconds they required to fully heal up. Now, however, they constituted the final obstacle to my reaching the church, whose outline I could just make out on the western horizon.

As the vile wankers finished off the kraut, I turned my rifle on them before they could turn their massacring ways on me. The only sound I heard, however, was a loud clicking to indicate that my rifle was empty. It also seemed that my clipper was now bereft of further ammunition. Realizing I had to act quickly I detached the bayonet and charged at the two.

My first swipe took off the top of the injured one's skull, causing what constituted its brains to plop out onto the German soldier's mutilated form. I then stood up and pointed my blade at the second, fully intact reanimate. This one looked particularly regal even in death, its pale features and unkempt salt and pepper-colored hair being quite notable.

DORIAN GRAY VS. REANIMATOR
Attack of the Dead Men
Christofer Nigro

The thing's widely glaring eyes looked at me through a barrel of wrath, as if it had just caught me playing hide the meat with its mom or daughter.

The tattered uniform this one wore with the distinctive gold buttons could be readily identified as an *Uhlan* of Prussian royalty. This suggested that while living he was a man of rank; it was a status that his – for some reason I was no longer thinking of him as an *it* – current state of being almost seemed to recall on some primordial, subconscious level. Or, whatever passes for that in these reanimated carcasses to whom Herbert's chemical grants a most crude semblance of restored life.

The dead madman's mouth opened wide and released a horrific sound resembling a hybrid of a moan and a shout as he raised the kraut's filched rifle in preparation for using it like a bludgeon on me.

I shouted back at him with a considerably more articulate threat of violence to come. "Let's go, mate! You and me, right here! I'll cut you to pieces before you get the chance to shove that rifle at me, whether inside an existing orifice or in an attempt to create a new one!"

This was when I noticed a subtle whooshing noise many meters above us. I looked up to see an enormous cigar-shaped behemoth coasting upwards in the dark starry sky.

"Oh, bloody hell. A Zeppelin! I really do hate those."

The reanimate likewise peered upwards and a distinct look of fear crossed his pallid visage as if he could still recognize and sense what havoc that massive hovering purveyor of death was about to unleash upon us.

"Every bastard for himself!" I yelled as I turned and ran towards the closest shelter I could find.

The reanimate appeared to turn and do so as well, though in the opposite direction.

It was too late, however. We had evidently been spotted by some bloke in the dirigible with binoculars, and a three-ton bomb was dropped on us. The familiar sound it made while whistling through the air was utterly terrifying to the ears of anyone who knew what was to follow – and I was admittedly no exception.

The resulting explosion was huge, and I could feel my eardrums burst like miniature balloons stuck with a pin as everything turned to fire around me.

***

I am not certain how much time had passed when I finally awakened, but my shattered eardrums, along with multiple burns on my skin and pulverized internal organs, had all been healed up. I looked around to see that the Zeppelin was long gone, its crew no doubt thinking that the explosive had done its deadly job. No sign of the reanimate was evident, so I figured that the regal-looking dead chap must have been blasted to bits, perhaps too small and dispersed to recognize as human debris without a thorough inspection of the ground.

I stepped out of the huge crevice left in the earth by the bomb and looked to the east of me in dismay. The Le Translov Church where the Huns had gathered their spoils from raiding Vaast's abbey in Arras had been largely reduced to rubble by the blast, much as the original had been earlier in the war. I tried not to despair, though, since I had heard rumors that the bones and vials of the saint were hidden in a thick metal chest that could likely survive such a shelling.

I ran the rest of the distance toward the remains of the church, able to see my surroundings better since dawn was now aborning. I walked through the crumbled infrastructure until I found the chest. It was obviously the one I was seeking, for the symbol of Vaast's coat of arms, a Teutonic Knight slaying a giant bird with a sword, was engraved on it. However, the lid had been opened and its contents removed. Had the Germans become aware of what treasures it beheld and taken them for use by the Central Powers?

"Damn it all!" I shouted as I kicked the thick metal casket in frustration.

I then had to sit and wait for my broken middle toe to heal up before I could comfortably begin my two-mile walk back to Herbert's shoddy base of operations to report that our mission was an abject failure… and to have a word with him about the excesses of the assistance he provided.

***

There is a detail to this incident that I was only to learn about later, something that occurred almost an hour before I awakened following the Zeppelin bombing. If I had recovered from my "mortal" injuries earlier I would have seen the final "surviving" reanimate trudging towards the remains of the church, having apparently weathered the massive explosion better than I had. He stumbled more or less aimlessly through the rubble, almost as if unerringly guided by some outside "signal."

The walking dead man came across the chest containing St. Vaast's bones and other implements, including a few vials holding his legendary chemical vapors. This container had indeed been strong enough to weather the blast, but the lock on its lid had been broken by a heavy fragment of granite that fell from one of the building's towers during the explosion.

The glassy-eyed reanimate picked up one of the saint's leg bones and looked it over with an expression of great curiosity. He then lifted one of the vials, glared at the murky contents of the transparent glass, and impulsively pulled the blocker out of the top. This was followed by the walking cadaver howling in what appeared to be a combination of shock and agony as iridescent green vapors billowed out the bottle's opening and were absorbed into his mouth, nostrils, ears, and pores.

The figure slumped to his knees as the ancient alchemical brew of St. Vaast interacted with the modern reagent injected into his veins by the good Dr. West… and the reanimate began changing.

***

Dr. Herbert West was calmly mixing some of his latest chemical components when I burst into his cabin.

"Welcome back, Dorian," he said with no discernible tone. "You look quite good for a man who just strolled through trenches filled with armed German soldiers, a horde of my reanimates, and… that was a bomb I heard dropped from a Zeppelin just over an hour ago, correct?"

I clasped my fists and gritted my teeth, barely able to hold my temper in check. My rifle had been emptied but I had the formerly attached bayonet in my hand, its gleaming blade covered in the dried blood of living and dead men alike.

23

DORIAN GRAY VS. REANIMATOR
Attack of the Dead Men
Christofer Nigro

"Yes, I am fully intact, Herbert. No thanks to your going over the top with that reagent of yours!"

"That was the plan, was it not? I had warned you of the danger, and you got there and back as expected. But I see no cargo in your hands. Did the mission fail?"

"It did, but it may not have if you had only injected just enough cadavers instead of an entire legion of them. As a result, they – including a particularly spry member of their lot – prevented me from reaching the church before that damned dirigible had dropped its load. Vaast's chest of treasures had been pilfered by the time I awakened and could search the remains of the cathedral."

"It had? I thought the krauts were unaware that the Huns had stored Vaast's remains in that other church."

"Someone bloody well knew about it. And someone bloody well took the goods before I could procure them for our purposes. All because you could not control your zealous use of that infernal chemical of yours."

I lifted my blade in a threatening fashion. Yes, Herbert had overperformed to my detriment, but much of this was indeed my own blame as the plan was mine to begin with. Nevertheless, I was much too angry at the time for such self-introspection. I wanted blood for going through so much only to lose such a potentially valuable treasure to unseen hands.

My newest friend turned and saw my menacing gesture. He calmly put a vial he was working with back on the counter and loudly clapped his hands together. That sound summoned four reanimates from the back of the room that awkwardly but quickly moved to the scientist's side as if acting as bodyguards. Each had a very distinctive circular burn mark on their foreheads, making it obvious what procedure Herbert had put them through while I was out and about in the trenches. This man was nothing if not prepared for the eventuality of my turning on him had the mission gone south.

"Do calm down and back off, Dorian. I know you're good with a blade, but these four non-living gentlemen will tear into you with brutal abandon if I give the signal. And not even your skills may be enough to overcome this number of them.

"Further, there is also the matter of this syringe in my possession that is filled with a very toxic poison." He lifted the glass implement containing a mustard-colored fluid to verify that he spoke no idle threat. "You may cut one or even two of them to pieces during the skirmish, Lieutenant D. Gray, but the other two will surely rip your arms and legs off. Can you regenerate entire limbs?"

I could certainly grow back pieces of flesh and brain cells... including, as I learned tonight, an ear lobe. But at this time, I honestly had no idea how long it would take me to regenerate entire limbs from a four-quarter dismemberment, nor from a potent poison loosed in my bloodstream. And that was not to mention anything else Herbert might choose to cut off when I was in recovery stasis. In short, I would be at his perverse mercy if I lost this fight, making me think that I needed to pick the when and how of this eventual conflict.

"There will be a next time, Herbert," I told him with a quiet but firm demeanor. "We immortals have all the time in the world. So, have a care."

"I advise you to do the same, my friend. Because you never know when I may learn the secrets of immortality my own way, after which I may very well confer upon both me and others of my choosing who will be in solemn debt to me as a result. And know that I will never cease being curious about how a professionally rendered portrait has given you such a perfect version of the gift I am seeking to create for mankind with the bio-chemical sciences."

"Continue fantasizing about any scenario you wish, Herbert. Just be aware that life is not a game, and I am apt to be at it far longer than you, or any person who may undergo some 'treatment' of yours, either today or in the distant future. Good day, now."

I then calmly walked out of the hut, leaving the doctor to continue his unholy experiments while doing a good amount of unholy planning of my own. We would doubtless meet again, and when we did... well, I wagered that the outcome may well not be to his liking.

***

The Prussian House of Representatives, Berlin – Six months later

This is a post-script to my journal of events that I would discover much later. They describe an event stemming from the chapter told above that would come back to haunt me, my new friend Herbert West... and the rest of the world in due course.

Oberleutnant Hans Kimmler sat on a plush chair in the office he was recently awarded in the Empire's main parliamentary building, smoking an imported Austrian stogie and practicing exhaling the smoke in rings as he looked out the twin windows behind his desk at the streets two stories below him. He felt powerful and above the masses as he believed one of his station should, wondering if his recent honored promotion was the only life-changing gift that All-Father Wotan could bequeath to him.

That musing was answered when his door was suddenly pushed open. The high-ranking officer was startled, to say the least, when he turned to see that the man who had the temerity to barge into his sanctuary without knocking was none other than *Uhlan* Gunter von Kriest – a man who was listed as one of the casualties of British artillery in the mean trenches.

The corporal did not look quite as Kimmler had remembered him, however. The skin on his face and hands was much paler than he recalled, and his eyes had gone from a bright blue to a dull overcast gray. His salt and pepper hair seemed to be sticking up in an unusual manner for men of his ranking and culture. He was grinning widely with his formerly pearly white teeth now bearing a sickly yellowish hue.

Otherwise, the man appeared robust, energetic, and quite alive. He was dressed in his familiar military regalia and was holding some item concealed in a thick cloth towel.

"*Mein Gott! Uhlan* von Kriest? I had heard that you were…?"

"Those reports were not altogether untrue, *Oberleutnant*," the corporal replied with a voice slightly scratchier than what his superior officer recalled. "You will understandably find it quite hard to believe what I have gone through over the past several months… and how I have changed. Nevertheless, I believe you will find the gift I have brought to you far more extraordinary than even the tale I have to tell."

Kimmler pulled his square-rimmed bifocals over his eyes and looked intently at the covered object in von Kriest's left hand. "You *do* indeed have much to explain. But before you do that tell me what it is that you bring me."

"I am most pleased you asked me that first, sir."

von Kriest's unsightly yellowed teeth were made all the more visible as he beamed widely before unwrapping the towel to reveal an old-fashioned looking vial filled with a viscous luminescent green liquid.

END

PORTRAIT OF A GRAY GIRL

Pete Rawlik

London, November 1918

It should have ended there, Pickman. I had my fill of Dorian Gray and his wanton ways to last my entire life. That a man with such gifts could waste them in such a manner was abhorrent to me. He had somehow obtained the state of near-immortality that I wished to bestow on mankind. Not all humans, as that would be ruinous, but to the best and the brightest, to the artists and scientists and great statesmen heretofore cut down at the height of their greatness; it is to *these* men I would offer my gift. They would use it well to create works of genius, to advance the sciences, to sculpt a listening and grand society.

Dorian has somehow gained this very gift and all he does with it is wallow in the various pleasures of the flesh, wasting what he has been given. Even the war and his newfound sense of patriotism failed to reform him. I was glad to be rid of him.

Imagine my surprise when he found me in London.

It was late November of 1918, I was through with the wilds of England, and resigned myself to staying in London for just a few more days before heading back to the continent. I was planning on visiting the region straddling the border of Spain and Portugal to research one of the many legends that Dorian had mentioned to me. I had not been a believer in the various preternatural tales of monstrous immortals, but Dorian Gray and what I had seen him do

29

changed all that. If one such as he existed then perhaps there were other things like him, things that might help me in my attempt to perfect the science of reanimation.

I was in the Grenville Library at the British Museum, perusing a copy of the biography of the Earl of Marsden, when a figure sat down opposite me and in a rather whimsical voice greeted me. "Good morning to you, Doctor Herbert West."

I looked up and knew immediately that it was him. He wasn't dressed as a soldier anymore; he was more of an effete dandy, attired in a white suit with a matching overcoat and hat. I will admit his outfit amazed me; not its design or cut, but rather the fact that somehow Dorian Gray had avoided getting a single bit of muck or dust on it. London had not earned the nickname The Great Smoke for its cleanliness. But somehow, Dorian in this entirely impractical outfit had managed to create an astounding feat of luxuriant cleanliness, of ivory sterility unrivalled by even the most fastidious of surgeries.

I rolled my eyes and sighed in frustration. "Dorian Gray, what an unpleasant surprise. How exactly did you find me?"

"When you are my age, you have your ways. Many people all across the Empire owe me favors. Tracking you down was a trifle, really."

He reached out to touch my hand, but I recoiled in disgust.

"Aren't you pleased to see me, Herbert? You should be. I come bearing gifts."

"I am as pleased to see you, Dorian, as Polyphemus was to encounter Odysseus." I closed my book.

He snorted, "How very droll, Herbert; how very droll, indeed."

And then there was some dread, an unmeasured length of silence between us that I eventually felt forced to interrupt. "Well, what is it?"

"Eh," he seemed suddenly distant or distracted.

DORIAN GRAY VS. REANIMATOR
Portrait of a Gray Girl
Pete Rawlik

"You said you came bearing gifts. What exactly are you giving me, Dorian?"

"Ah, yes. What I am giving you, Herbert," he said as he slid a card across the table, "is opportunity."

I looked at the small, pale rectangle of cardstock that he had offered me as if it were a viper or some other venomous creature. There was an address printed upon it. I will say that it was a home somewhere in London, but propriety prevents me from revealing any more details than that. Cautiously I picked it up, as it was, after all, just a fancy piece of paper. Then I slid it back.

"No, Dorian, I don't think so. Whatever it is you want from me, the answer is, and always shall be, no."

The everlastingly young man stood up and at the same time slid the card back in my direction. "You don't trust me, Herbert, and I understand that. I have no right to expect that you would. But there are things beyond the disagreements that keep us at odds. Something is happening, Herbert; something terrible. You need to see it for yourself, and once you do... well, we shall see what you do then." He tapped the card with a gloved hand once, and then again. "Go and see, Herbert; go and see."

Then he turned and strode out of the library. People scattered out of his way, scurrying from his path like cockroaches from the light, as if he owned the place. And I was left there staring at this dreadful piece of paper with this terrible feeling that all eyes in the library were on me, wondering what exactly I was going to do.

My decision was inevitable. Dorian knew it would be. And so, after a quiet bite to eat, I found myself traversing the streets of London and standing at the gate of one of the many estates that had been swallowed up by the city. It was not a vast property, but the wall was tall enough, and the gardens thick enough to prevent me from seeing the house from the street.

DORIAN GRAY VS. REANIMATOR
Portrait of a Gray Girl
Pete Rawlik

I rang the bell and waited. Within a few moments, a slim woman with a rather dour face came out to the gate, a large ring of keys dangling from her hand. "You are Doctor West?"

I indicated that I was.

"We've been expecting you." And then the gate creaked open after the key was inserted.

I stepped through and then the woman swung the metal barrier shut and locked it tight after I had entered. "I am the housekeeper, Miss Hartill."

She was in her mid-thirties, rather tall and thin. Her hair was iron gray and neatly tucked into a bun. There was something about her that suggested that she was an educator, a schoolteacher, or perhaps a headmistress. These impressions may have been formed due to the manner in which she carried herself, or the tone in which she spoke. It was the voice of authority.

The strange woman led me to a house that had seen better days. The brickwork was stained and cracked, while the paint around the window frames was faded and flaked. Some of the panes were cracked or missing and patched up with boards. As we went in, the front door made a dull scraping sound, and I could smell the distinctive aroma of woodworm in the hall.

She led me into a sitting room and told me to wait. It was large and well-lit. There were about ten large photographs in ornate frames, all of the same young girl with different women. Or so I thought at first.

The first image was of a girl aged about ten years. I suppose she would have been considered a lovely young woman. She was fair of skin and hair, with remarkably penetrating eyes and delicate hands. A middle-aged woman wearing a black dress and a white apron held one of those hands tightly.

DORIAN GRAY VS. REANIMATOR
Portrait of a Gray Girl
Pete Rawlik

To the far side was another child, another girl. This one not so pretty or fair, she was a bit younger than the other, and a bit rougher. You could see it in the eyes. Clutched in her hands was a porcelain doll which seemed quite new and finely made, though the details of it escaped me as the face was held toward the child's body. A small brass placard embedded at the base of the frame was engraved with what I supposed was the year of the photograph, 1877.

The same child appeared in the next image. Different were the styles of clothing and hair, but the shape of her face was the same and she still had those same piercing eyes. Next to her was a woman in her twenties, rather tall and thin with thick glasses. I thought perhaps that the tag was in error for it was dated 1880, but in my estimation, the child had not aged one bit.

Third was a photograph of the same two people. Again, the child was made up in a different outfit, with different clothes and hair, but had not aged in any noticeable way. In contrast, the young woman was no longer young, and she was no longer attractive. Her eyes were sad, her hair bedraggled and showing signs of white. Nearly translucent, her skin seemed almost like paper. The brass placard was dated 1885, but given the appearance of age with the woman, whom I assumed was supposed to be a nanny, I would have thought it a much later date. An elaborate joke, I thought to myself.

Next was a portrait dated 1887. In this example, the nanny was sitting in a wooden chair and seemed to have that look that women get when they are very tired, suffering from anemia, or perhaps consumption. In contrast, the young lady was bright, almost cheerful. She even had a pleasant smile on her face.

The one after that was rather startling. In it, the young lady was dressed in an all-black, formal outfit and carrying a small bouquet of flowers. Behind her to the side sat the nanny, this time in a large, overstuffed chair. She too was dressed in black, with only a frill of white at her neck where the collar snuck out. The woman had a sad frightened look about her. She didn't appear old, at least not much older than she had before, but rather used up; and again, there was in my mind the suggestion of consumption or perhaps even cancer.

Her hands were wizened and claw-like and one rested on the arm of the chair. The other held the girl-child's hand. No, that's not true, she didn't so much hold her hand as grip it, and not the hand proper, but at the wrist. It was as if she was forcing one's attention to the child's hand. I knew immediately that there was something amiss, but it took me a moment or two to realize what exactly was wrong.

In the picture, the child's hand was broken, to be precise the thumb of her left hand was missing beyond the joint. One would have thought that the loss would have left behind a scarred-over, lumpy mound of flesh, but instead, it was jagged and sharp like a broken branch or shard of glass. The date was 1891.

"Her name is Emily," Dorian Gray whispered in my ear. I had been so absorbed by my examination of the photos that I hadn't heard him come in. "Don't let me interrupt. Please continue your perusal of her portraits."

He set a large hatbox down and then began taking off his coat.

The next photograph was of the perpetual girl – Emily – and was dated 1893. Here, the new nanny was of Hindu origin and by all appearances seemed quite stern. I looked to Emily's right hand and saw that even more of the thumb had been lost, but that a prosthetic of leather had been strapped in its place.

What followed then was an assortment of photographs in rapid chronological succession. There were five taken over the course of six years, if I recall correctly, all with different women, and all showing a slow progression of the deterioration of Emily's left hand. A joint or finger, a portion of the palm, another finger, more of the palm, until finally by the year 1900 the entire hand was gone, and replaced by a jointed, wooden prosthetic.

From then on, the pictures seemed to have been commissioned on an annual basis, documenting more than a dozen nannies over the course of nearly two decades. More importantly, they showed something much more interesting than a change in domestics.

In each portrait, there was evidence of a minuscule but steady state of decay in Emily's body. The hand was just the beginning; 1903's depiction showed that most of her lower right leg was gone, and by 1907 the lobe of her right ear as well, which progressed in 1910 to the loss of the entire ear. 1912's image showed her sitting in a chair without either of her legs. By 1915 the whole left arm was gone. In 1917 her right arm was missing up to the elbow.

"Is she like you?" I asked while looking at Dorian.

He was sitting in a large chair, his damned white suit still as clean as the driven snow, the hatbox, an ornate item with gold-colored panels and silver leaf, sat on his lap. "Yes and no, Herbert. Yes and no."

I sat down in the chair across from him. "You will, of course, elaborate," I said as I crossed my legs and tapped my foot gently on the rug.

Dorian sighed in obvious frustration. "I thought, as a Doctor, you would have a more deductive mind. Everything you need to know is in those paintings."

"The nannies, they seem depleted. Does she drain them somehow?"

"No, no, not at all. You are correct that she goes through them at a rather brisk pace but there is no malevolence on her part there. I have seen the same symptoms in my own companions. I think there is perhaps something debilitating in being in close proximity to our kind. Perhaps we burn too brightly, and the fires of life, being unable to consume us, instead consume those who linger too close, and too long."

He laughed at this. "As I said, she is akin to me, we share some history in common, but there are variances in our origins. It is these variances that engender stark differences in our current conditions." There was a hint of sadness or perhaps melancholy in his voice.

"The artist who painted your portrait... he painted Emily as well."

"Yes." He rested one hand on top of the hatbox.

I looked around at the photographs. "When she was a child."

"Yes." He undid the clasp of the side of the hatbox. "She was but ten years old in 1877, when this all began for her."

"If she were ten in 1877, then..." I ran the numbers in my head. "She's been trapped in the body of a child for more than forty years."

Dorian made a sound affirming my conclusion. The box opened from the side, and he stared sadly at the contents.

"You were painted on canvas." I looked back at the portraits. "But Emily was painted on something less durable." I stood up and walked over to 1891. "This decay, the degeneration of the various body parts... whatever Emily's portrait was done on, it's breaking down. That is why she's losing pieces of herself. But..."

"But what, my good doctor?"

"The decay isn't random. If she were painted on a canvas or piece of vellum or parchment, the decay would spread from the edges inward. But this is more like it's spreading from points of damage, like an infection, like gangrene." I spun around and looked at my host. "You said everything I need to know was in the pictures."

Dorian nodded, "Indeed I did."

I walked slowly back to the first portrait. The one with two girls, one on either side of the nanny, and suddenly as I stared at it, I understood.

"Emily's portrait was painted on the doll, the porcelain doll!"

"Yes, well done, Herbert. I knew you wouldn't disappoint."

"A present, for a birthday, perhaps?"

"Yes."

"And then what? Rejected? Outgrown? Given away to her friend, the daughter of the nanny?"

"Go on."

"All this before anyone understood what was happening."

Dorian's voice was full of sadness. "They thought she was just slow to develop and blamed the nanny for not taking care of her properly. Sacked the woman, sent her packing, and her daughter along with her."

"With the doll?" It was both a question and a statement.

"With the doll." I heard Dorian stand up behind me. "It was years, more than a decade of doctors poking and prodding her, before they had any clue of what the true nature of her condition was. Can you imagine, ten years of not knowing, and then…?"

"Her thumb breaks off, and it all becomes clear… well, clearer."

"Her parents began searching for answers immediately, but it was already too late. By then the painter, my good friend Basil Hallward, was dead. They traced the nanny to India, dead of cholera, and the child, to Australia, in service herself. The girl barely remembered the doll. Her last memory of it is in a manor house in Scotland, but she could have lost it anywhere on three continents."

"It was loved, at least up until 1891, and probably well looked after for some time after that," I suggested.

"What makes you say that?" Dorian wondered.

DORIAN GRAY VS. REANIMATOR
Portrait of a Gray Girl
Pete Rawlik

"The rate of breakage. After the thumb was broken, it took almost a decade for the rest of the hand to follow. It may have been repaired in some way or another. Whatever the case, the damage was slowed for some time."

"And then?"

I walked back to the later images. "Cast aside, in some child's forgotten toy box, or in a rubbish tip somewhere. The latter I think, based on the progressive damage. These sudden losses and breaks are likely from more material being piled on top, additional weight crushing the limbs."

"Well done, my dear Doctor West. It took you some time to become engaged, but once you were, you performed admirably. Your conclusions are comparable to those we made many years ago."

"We?" I asked, turning around.

And then I saw it, and it spoke to me. I ran, Richard. I ran from that house and out the gate and into the streets of London. I ran until I couldn't run anymore, until my lungs burned, and my legs felt like they were going to fall off. And after that I left London as soon as I could. I had to get away, you see; had to get away from the thing in that house. The thing that Dorian Gray tended to. The thing in the hatbox.

Do you know what it was, Richard? It was Emily. Both her ears were gone, and some of her teeth, and part of her lower jaw. One of her eyes had gone dull. She looked at me and grinned a mad kind of smile with what teeth she had left.

Although it was Emily, it was just her head. *Just her head!* Can you imagine that? Can you imagine the horror of living like that? Trapped and immobile, perhaps for decades? And then she spoke to me, and her words filled me with terror and dread.

"Is this the gift you would impart to mankind, Doctor West?" she asked. "Is this the life you would condemn us to?"

And as I fled, I could hear Dorian Gray laugh.

DORIAN GRAY VS. REANIMATOR
Portrait of a Gray Girl
Pete Rawlik

END

STILL LIFE WITH THE UNDEAD

Pete Rawlik

Winter 1921

I want to begin by thanking you, Richard. There are but a handful of people I deem to call friend, but I am pleased to number you among them. When I cabled you in January, I never expected the lengths you would have to go to return me to New England. Even so, I must admit that the predicament I continue to find myself in is particularly delicate and engenders a significant burden on you. Unfortunately, I must ask you for still more assistance than you have already rendered.

Don't look at me like that. I need you, Pickman, as I'm hardly in any condition to help myself. I haven't since that night more than a year ago. What did the papers call it? The Sefton Asylum Massacre. It was the night that Clapham-Lee broke out Halsey, and the two of them, and a legion of others, attacked me. Unjustly, mind you. They had no right. No right at all. And no right to do what they did next, either.

They scattered me to the four corners of the Earth, Pickman. I don't know where, but I can still *feel them* – my limbs and my torso, they're out there somewhere. I've read reports of amputees still suffering feeling in lost limbs – "phantom pain," they call it. My remote sensing of my limbs must be something like that. It goes to support my theory, that while the center of consciousness resides in the brain, vestiges of that awareness are spread throughout the body.

40

DORIAN GRAY VS. REANIMATOR
Still Life with the Undead
Pete Rawlik

Even in London, I could feel my limbs and torso being moved, the distances between us growing ever greater. Clapham-Lee must have known about this, perhaps even experimented with his own body to study the phenomenon. It is my theory that if the various anatomical parts are closer, they might even be able to be spontaneously drawn to each other and that this factor is only neutralized after a considerable distance. I suspect that this is why Clapham-Lee absconded with me, or at least my head, to London, while the rest of me were shipped to parts unknown.

Clapham-Lee thought this punishment enough for my supposed sins, and he arranged for me to make use of his property known as Agar House, on Harley Street. It was there that I set up practice, assisted by one Doctor Levi Hip, and together we began catering to a rather distinct clientele. We were only a few doors away from the famed Edward Bach and thus benefitted from his presence. Like myself, Bach was unsatisfied with the state of modern medicine and sought alternative methods of treatment.

Of course, it was Hip that did much of the actual work, albeit under my direction. The ruse, for obviously we needed one, was that I was a quadriplegic, and confined to a wheelchair. We set up a consulting room, filled with mirrors, magnifying devices, and projectors… such that whatever part of a patient Doctor Hip was examining I was readily able to see it as well, even from the relative safety behind my desk.

I suspected that Levi Hip was not my new associate's real name and that he was possessed of some terrible secret that, were it to be revealed, could ruin him; or perhaps had already ruined his true identity. Regardless, he was an adequate physician, and with my help, we soon gained a reputation for professionalism and medical skill. That we had hired members of the public to spread rumors concerning our capabilities had certainly paid off. It did not take long at all

41

for the reputation of Herbert and Hip to be firmly established.

Within a month of opening our offices, we were soon consulting with a number of other practices and being visited by the strangest of clients, which we encouraged, as long as they could pay – in one manner or another. It has been my experience that information, and a feeling of indebted gratitude is often more valuable than any coin of the realm. By the autumn of 1921, we were so prosperous that I was even able to renew my research into the reanimation of the dead, with Hip's assistance, of course.

Meanwhile, I had accumulated a small but regular network of agents dispersed throughout the British Empire. From these, I received regular reports. The primary purpose was the search for the wayward portions of my body, but my instructions were vague enough that I consistently received accounts concerning all manner of outré events.

And then one cool November morning I received a missive from one of my most trusted agents. It suggested that several of my London-based instruments had been interfered with. Not killed, mind you, but rather reassigned suddenly, without warning, and shipped overseas with such rapidity that they had not even been granted the time to write a letter to inform me thus. It represented a bold stroke against me which hinted that perhaps some government agency or criminal cabal had taken notice of my affairs.

I soon learned that the action was initiated by something – someone - far more insidious.

It was like any other day, and he was scheduled just like any other patient. His paperwork claimed that he was suffering from a generalized malaise, and I expected to prescribe what I normally recommended for such things, a mild infusion of cocaine. Imagine my surprise when our nurse brought in our next patient, whom I recognized immediately as Dorian Gray!

DORIAN GRAY VS. REANIMATOR
Still Life with the Undead
Pete Rawlik

"Hello, Herbert," he said in that cloying voice he regularly used, which made my teeth clench. "It has been some time since we have seen each other."

"Not long enough, Dorian," I hissed back at him.

My unexpected guest chuckled in his usual boyish manner and sat down in a chair, crossing his legs. He wore a suit of pale yellow, a color fashionable since the war had ended, with a dragon-headed walking stick in his left hand. "I must say, you're looking surprisingly well for a man in your condition. I had heard rumors of your demise."

"Wildly exaggerated. My expiration was only temporary in nature."

"Although not without certain costs, I see."

Doctor Hip was obviously confused. "I'm sorry," he said, "this seems to be some long-standing personal disagreement. Should I leave?"

"Yes," said Dorian.

"No," I countered. "Have a seat. Dorian won't be staying for long."

"Well," he exclaimed, "you are correct on that point. I won't be here for long. Just long enough."

"Long enough for what?"

"Doctor Herbert West, the last time we met I warned you about the dangers you might face, the consequences that might occur if you continued your experiments into reanimation. I even showed you an example of what could go wrong, if you weren't careful with the application of your formula."

"How is Emily?" I asked.

Dorian scowled at me. "We lost her last year. Wherever the china doll was, it finally succumbed to the pressures around it."

"You have my sympathies."

"We do not want your sympathies, Herbert. We wanted to make you understand. There are risks associated with the research you undertake, unknowable side effects, and as you have seen, terrible personal tragedies. Now you suffer through the very nightmare that you ran screaming from! Trapped, immobile, and living a half-life, yet you still continue your studies? Have you no shame?"

I laughed at him, a rich and malignant laugh, both mocking and mephitic. "You are such a fool, Dorian. You sit there with your perpetual youth and good looks, and you surround yourself with lesser versions of yourself, so afraid that whatever forces granted you such a gift might run out or be used up. You're so terrified that it is *you* who have become immobile, unwilling, and unable to research your condition, and perhaps resolve your status." I took an angry breath. "I am a scientist, Dorian, and while you seem content to suffer the inevitable, I have done something about it."

Hip stood up and raised his hands in supplication. "Herbert, I don't think this is the right time."

"You don't think?" My voice was raised. "You don't think at all! Where would you be without my genius?"

I then rose up from my wheelchair, grabbed a scalpel from the instrument table, and in a swift and singular motion, slit Doctor Levi Hip's throat.

He instantly fell to his knees, his hand clawing at the blood that was spurting from the severed arteries, his mouth making useless gurgling noises. Hip looked at me with pleading eyes, but I ignored his last desperate acts.

Instead, I threw off the black cloak that was wrapped around me and revealed myself to Dorian Gray.

"I have studied, Dorian! I have studied and *learned*. And while my own body and limbs may be denied to me, this is London, the home of Jack the Ripper and the Thames Torso Murderer. I found substitutes. The grafting took a while to perfect, but I assure you that it is more than up to the task of confronting you and your holier-than-thou attitude."

It was only then, in the bright light of the consulting room, with the mirrors and magnifiers and projectors, that I saw what I had become, what I had made of myself. I was a patchwork man. A ragtag collection of body parts held together by catgut sutures and metal pins. I was a monster in all senses of the word, and my thoughts drifted immediately to the failures of Victor Frankenstein more than a century earlier.

I brought the bloody scalpel up to my eyes and looked at it, along with the hand that held the implement. It was a parody of a hand, sewn together from the bits and pieces of dozens of others, and then reanimated with my own reagent. The whole body was like that, and it was only through sheer force of will that I could maintain control over the grafted madness I had created. I turned and looked at Dorian, and he saw the insanity and self-loathing seeping into my eyes.

"Let us put a stop to this right now," he said rising from his chair.

In a graceful arc, he twisted the head of his cane and drew forth a short sword. Before I even knew what was happening, I had been cut a half dozen times. My limbs and torso crumpled beneath me; the sutures that held them together sliced clean. Another cut and my head rolled free.

I gave a brief squeal that might have led to a scream, but Dorian was having none of it. He scooped up my cloak, shoved a ball of it into my mouth, and wrapped the rest about my head.

I can only assume that we exited the building via the back door, for within seconds I knew we were inside an automobile and speeding away down the street. We travelled for quite some time, but Dorian remained silent the entire trip. I could hear the traffic and noise of the city but had no idea where I was being taken.

It was only later when we exited the automobile and ventured inside a building that he removed the cloth and let me see where he had taken me. Is it any surprise that it was the same house of horrors that I had fled a few years earlier? I was there, in the sitting room surrounded by the images of Emily, her enchanting eyes staring down at me. My captor sat me down on a tray atop a small table in the middle of the room and stood back to look at me.

"Damn you, Dorian! Just what are your intentions?"

"My intentions, Herbert? My intentions are to teach you a lesson, to make you understand once and for all."

With that, he turned, and I saw what was in his hands: it was the ornate hatbox that had once housed the sad remains of the doll-child Emily. Dorian stalked over and before I could protest, I was encased inside. From my new prison, I could see nothing, but I could hear; and what I heard suggested that I was being boxed up inside a wooden crate.

"This isn't permanent, Herbert," dictated Dorian, "but I'm hoping this temporary incarceration will be educational."

Then I heard the hammer strike the frame repeatedly and everything went quiet. And the complete silence continued for what seemed like an eternity.

You must understand, Pickman, that I was imprisoned in that box for weeks. I suppose after the first day or so, there was no real way for me to tell time and I went a little mad. I saw things, imagined things, strange and terrible things. I have committed horrific acts in my quest for the secrets of immortality, but everything I had previously done paled in comparison to what I saw and heard there in the darkness.

Dorian was right; my imprisonment was needed. And it *did* change me, for I *did* learn something. Only it wasn't what he had expected.

All those days in the quiet dark, all those things that I imagined I saw and heard. They've made me realize that I had been wrong about how I was approaching my studies. I need to change my direction and my tactics. I need to become even more dedicated, with a focus on more significant progress. It may sound ruthless and depraved, but I need to find a way to perfect my reagent, no matter what the cost to myself or those around me!

What? Yes, I know I said that Dorian took me from Hip in November. Why did I wait until January to cable you? Where was I for those two months? What was I doing? I would rather not speak of it.

Now, Pickman, we have much work to do. We must find the rest of my body, and perhaps some of your colleagues can help with that. Then we must find someone skilled enough to put me back together.

Well, one thing at a time.

END

FROM A DEAD SOLDIER

Christofer Nigro

Dorian Gray's Private Journal. London, Mid-January 1922

I rushed into the lavish home I had rented on London's West End in a state of near euphoria. I learned that one somewhat dear to my heart whom I believed lost to me for good had hope to walk among us once again.

Before that story could be told, however, I must first make note of another, one that had to occur in order for the above tale to be possible. With much reluctance, but so elated that my regret was much less than one might think, I sauntered towards the old hatbox that contained the disembodied head of one Dr. Herbert West.

I lifted the top to see the perpetually living and thinking head appearing to do neither of the above. Covered with a mop of white hair that now truly needed the care of a barber, Herbert's head had its eyelids clamped shut and made no sound. The scientist was clearly lost in thought, of the sort that only the severely sensory deprived could achieve. I would ordinarily have been pleased to leave him in such a state indefinitely... but I now needed him awake and cognizant once more.

"West!" I said loudly while tapping him atop his skull with the rigid index finger of my white-gloved hand. When the head failed to respond, I poked it harder and reiterated his name even louder than before.

"Huuhhah!" was the closest I can phonetically render the sound that he made when his eyes and mouth popped open in tandem.

His pale blue irises darted frantically about the room that was lit only by the sunlight barely streaming in through the closed curtains of the windows. The doctor's mouth remained gaping wide until his gaze fixed on me, and a semblance of cogency seemed to return to the bodiless visage.

"Dorian...?"

"Yes, Herbert, it is me," I replied, matter-of-factly. "Welcome back to the land of the conscious."

"What is... where is...?"

"You are exactly where you were nearly two months previous when I put the lid over the hatbox where your head now resides. Take a few moments if you must to regain your bearings and readjust to rational thought, but do so quickly, as I need your brain at full capacity."

To his credit, Herbert did not stay on the periphery of incoherency for long. He quickly forced himself back to sharing time and space with images from the world we jointly called reality. Cheers to the stubborn brain of this expert of a damnable science. But it was a horrifying expertise that I regretfully and desperately needed at the moment.

"Dorian! The things I saw... horrible but illuminating! *So very illuminating!* If only I had the words to adequately share them with..."

"Share them another time, Herbert! And with one who actually cares to hear of them, if such company ever comes your way. Right now, I require you to carry out a task that perhaps only your misbegotten science can accomplish. And one that will enable you to do actual good for an innocent soul rather than unleashing one perfidy after another upon the world with your reckless experimentation."

Herbert could clearly see that he was in no position to refuse. I understood just the same, however, that his devious mind would be continuously planning, and that I would have to help him get back on his feet, so to speak, before he could help me. It was not something I would have been willing to consider if the matter at hand were any less dire.

"What...? What do you require, Dorian? Let us... talk, shall we?"

However, before I could begin discussing the nefarious deal that I felt compelled to make, I was rudely interrupted. The front windows shattered from a barrage of bullets being fired through the glass. The projectiles were aimed with military precision and struck me in my torso and the throat. I flew back from the impact, which felt equivalent to the blast wave of a bomb dropped from a Zeppelin. I landed on an expensive ash burl inlay side table, smashing it into splinters and causing the few glass knickknacks on it to fall into broken shards on the hardwood floor.

Damned bastards, whoever they were! They would pay for this in both funds and blood!

For now, however, the only blood spattered about was my own, and I would lay there for an interminable period before I awakened with my flesh and organs no longer inundated with puncture wounds. Only the holes in my vintage white Viceroy shirt and pinstripe jacket still bore the perforations of the sucker salvo.

That pseudo-deadly assault was not the main problem when I awakened, however. What had been done was undone easily enough by the mysterious magic that imbues my hidden portrait. But what was not so straightforwardly reversed was the fact that Herbert's head had been purloined from the hatbox where it had been sequestered for the past two months. It was absconded by parties unknown and was likely the reason for such a brazen assault in broad daylight. It is sometimes astounding what liberties can be taken when the London fog surrounds the neighborhood like a cloud of gaseous pea soup. I doubt that anyone outside had seen a damned thing, and most likely pretended to hear nothing.

The cretinous culprits would not remain elusive for long, however. Nor would they get away with obtaining the services of Herbert West at my expense. These marauders likely had no idea whom they had suffused with lead. If they had, they would have buried my body a hundred feet beneath the ground rather than leaving it just lying there waiting for my portrait to work its arcane unraveling of their slaughter. Hence, they likely thought I was just some typical affluent dandy without recourse to the various connections and resources I can call upon.

Among the latter are a better than fine detective who was currently in my debt and possesses a wide array of resources all his own. He will help me track my friend the doctor, and the well-armed thieves shall learn that they are not the only ones capable of launching unpleasant surprises with a determinedly gory outcome.

***

What happened next, the details of which I added to my journal, were only to be uncovered by me at a later date. It then became easy enough for me to piece together precisely the scenario that ensued before I was to directly re-enter the events.

The bodiless head of Herbert West looked about a laboratory setting in the new location his abductors had brought him to. The scientist could see it was well-equipped, precisely the type of place he could – and often would – conduct his ungodly experiments within. He quickly surmised that this had been provided for his specific use and that someone other than me was determined to make a deal with him for his ghastly field of expertise.

This proved to be correct when the reanimated but fully cognizant form of *Ulan* Gunter von Kriest of the Prussian royal military emerged from the shadows in the back of the facility to greet his esteemed guest. The soldier was dressed in his finest ranking uniform and smiled to reveal his yellowing, unliving but still functional teeth. Stepping out behind him was his superior officer, *Oberleutnant* Hans Kimmler, who looked at the doctor's ambulant head with his one good eye glaring with morbid curiosity through his round monocle.

"*Gott im Himmel*, it is true," Kimmler whispered aloud to himself.

"Doctor Herbert West, I presume?" von Kriest said to the scientist's head.

"It is, unless you know of any other physician who has recently lost his body yet continues to speak," Herbert quipped wearily.

"Hah! Hah! I do not at the current time, Doctor West," the undead corporal retorted in a slightly hoarse rendition of a Prussian accent. "So, you are the man – or a portion thereof – whom I risked much to free from that silly English aristocrat who was no doubt keeping you as a curiosity to eventually display to others for coin."

"That is the truth of the matter," Herbert lied, not wanting to give away any factual information at this point in time to a mysterious benefactor who was not likely acting with altruistic motives. The scientist was in no position, to say the least, to give away any possible advantage he might have in what he realized might turn out to be a worse situation than the one he faced at my hands. "Who am I speaking to, and what can I do for you? You and your compatriot wear the uniforms of the Prussian forces."

DORIAN GRAY VS. REANIMATOR
From a Dead Soldier
Christofer Nigro

"*Ja,*" the walking dead officer replied. "This honorable officer of mine is *Oberleutnant* Hans Kimmler, and I am *Ulan* Gunter von Kriest. In case you have yet to notice, I am a recipient of your glorious reagent formulae. Hence, I have you to thank for bringing me back from a most inglorious death at the hands of the Allied forces during the war."

West's bodiless countenance took on an expression of eerie incredulity. "What? But that is not possible. You... you..."

"Shouldn't be speaking with full coherence, *ja,* Doctor?" von Kriest finished West's sentence with a yellow toothy grin. "Not exactly a typical result of your chemical's current formulation, let alone what my own scientists managed to come up with after a hasty examination of my own blood, eh?"

"But then how...?"

"My full cogency is not the result of your reagent alone," the officer explained. "Rather, it is a result of that and my unexpected contact with what you might call a much more ancient variation of your chemical brew. One created by a legendary miracle worker known as St. Vaast and hidden inside a church located in a war-torn hamlet called Le Translov."

Herbert was then hit with a full realization, including the previous mystery of who had taken the alchemist's bones and the remaining vials of his "sacred" fluid.

"I... see," the scientist forced himself to utter, trying to sound as reserved and stoic as possible. He was determined to seek any chance of finding a way to gain the upper hand on his new captor, one he suspected was far more dangerous than I, the former Lieutenant Dorian Gray. "And... may I surmise, sir, that you require my aid in figuring out how Vaast's precursor to my own reagent works, so that we may together uncover the secret of immortality for all whom you deem worthy of such a gift?"

DORIAN GRAY VS. REANIMATOR
From a Dead Soldier
Christofer Nigro

"Not actually, Doctor West," von Kriest spat with a lowered tone. "I am a soldier, and therefore a dispenser of death, not life. That is where my expertise lies, and your reagent is the key to creating soldiers like nothing before seen on the battlefield since the legendary berserkers that once served the armies of the ancient Teutons. They will be invincible and implacable, demanding no pay, no food, no protection from the elements, and they shall fear no man or weapon.

"These will be undead warriors that seek only to kill for its own sake. Their minds shall be so addled by the side effects of resurrection that their resulting insanity could crave nothing more nor less than the blood of any person they see before them. They would be an invaluable asset on any battlefield!"

"Really, now?" Herbert responded glumly while trying not to display a sense of disapproval. His intention was to go along until he found himself in a much better position. "How intriguing. I would do well to get on with this project of… ours, *Ulan* von Kriest. However, in my present condition…"

"Worry not about that!" von Kriest interjected, with a force taking his superior officer Kimmler aback. However, the *Oberleutnant* simply continued to listen to the lead taken by the talking dead man who, despite being of a lower rank, he had come to fear. "In return for your agreed-upon aid in creating a version of your reagent to create my mindless army of unliving soldiers, I shall do two things for you.

"One, I will immediately find you a temporary body to graft your head upon and use my scientists' own formulation of the reagent to bestow animation to it. This version is inferior to your own, and a cadaver inoculated with it first reacts much like your own, but eventually becomes increasingly necrotic and resumes true death. But that leads to the other boon I shall grant you.

DORIAN GRAY VS. REANIMATOR
From a Dead Soldier
Christofer Nigro

"That second one will be providing you with generous samples of my blood, which have traces of both your reagent and the version utilized by Vaast which, combined with your own, restored my reanimated form to full consciousness and complete recollection of my previous memories. With it, we can then surely find a more permanent body for your head."

"Or, "the doctor interjected, "at least a series of them until my real body parts can be recovered. As well as finding a means of perfecting my own reagent by studying the remnants of its predecessor by Vaast. For military purposes, of course."

"Right," von Kriest responded while Kimmler continued to look on as if suffering a loss of words.

"Then, by all means, I agree to your most generous deal," Herbert lied once again. "But first…"

"*Ja,* of course," von Kriest concurred. "Produce a temporary body for your head to rest upon and handle the mechanics of our task. My honored superior *Oberleutnant* Kimmler shall provide you with that."

"*Ahem.* I would most like to do so," Kimmler finally spoke up, "but the scientific crew I hired for you are… no longer with us. To prevent them from ever sharing what they learned, now that our troops successfully recovered, er, Doctor West's head, required some rather… extreme measures. Their bodies were tossed in the incinerator, as since the upper hierarchy of the People's Party will surely be searching for any sign of them, no, er, part of those men could be allowed to remain intact for such an occurrence."

"Oh, there is no worry about that, *Oberleutnant*," von Kriest assured his superior officer. "You are correct when you say that we cannot utilize nor leave reasonably intact anyone who may be missed. It would have to be someone with such a vile reputation that everyone, even their own surviving parents, would cheer to see them gone. Hence, to make my stated meaning clearer, it falls to you to provide

Doctor West with the body he needs in a *very literal fashion.*"

"Wait, you cannot—!" Unfortunately, Kimmler was slow to catch onto the meaning of von Kriest's words; consequently, he turned and reached for his holstered firearm too slowly, as well. Thus, he barely had time to draw it before the undead *Uhlan* shoved a bayonet clear through his heart.

The *Oberleutnant* coughed up a thick torrent of blood as his eyes rolled into his head and he fell to the floor. Since the soldiers who had retrieved Doctor West were sent to the task with the belief that what they were recovering was a valuable animatronic dummy's head from an eccentric English inventor, and then immediately re-assigned elsewhere, there were no guards present to aid Kimmler. Of course, so hated was he that they likely would have left him to his fate and then acceded to von Kriest's command as the next ranking officer anyway.

"As you can see, your new temporary body awaits having your head on its shoulders, my good doctor," von Kriest said with another of his unsettling, yellow-toothed smiles. "I have some supplies of our version of the reagent, and I need only bring in a single surgeon to graft your head onto that of the *Oberleutnant's* body and administer the injection. Then you shall be back on your feet – well, actually, on Kimmler's feet, but why quibble with such details?"

"I anxiously await the opportunity to work with you once I again possess a pair of feet, sir," was West's casual reply.

***

One week later…

"How goes the body, Doctor West?" von Kriest asked the scientist as the latter worked feverishly amidst a pile of

56

bubbling chemical beakers and cadavers in various states of condition.

"It is holding up reasonably well," the doctor replied while turning a bit awkwardly on a pair of legs not his own to face the dead but walking Prussian soldier. "The remnants of my own muscle memory stored in my cranial synapses were restored to me with minimal physical therapy required thanks to a combination of how the reagent works and the surgeon you hired following to the letter the instructions I gave him on reconnecting nerve endings. It is a shame you had to take the measures you did following the completion of the grafting procedure."

"Indeed, *mein guter arzt*. Bettini was a good surgeon. At least his usefulness did not come to an end with his life, thanks to your need for as many spare parts as we can find."

"But of course."

I need to kill this despicable miscreant and get out of here, Herbert no doubt mused to himself at this moment. *In the meantime, I will be more than pleased to take the samples of his blood for whatever traces of Vaast's chemicals can be found in it. I shall put that knowledge to better use than any under his direction ever would. Starting with keeping me on* someone's *feet until my real body parts can be recovered. If only Kimmler's form can hold together for just another day or two, for I almost got what I require from his lab. So, now all I need to concoct is a viable plan of dispatching von Kriest and escaping from this infernal place.*

"My forces have acquired some unusual cadavers for you, *mien freund*. I hope you have made the most of that in the connected lab containing the more outré specimens we procured. You said of the acquisitions you wanted, 'the stranger, the better.' Accordingly, I must insist that I see some major progress in your work soon."

"Yes, you most certainly have done that, sir, for which I am most appreciative. I likewise thank you for allowing me to retain Kimmler's head for… study. And you shall most certainly see the progress you demand. Rest assured that very soon now my entire plan shall come to fruition."

"You had best believe the good doctor," came an unexpected voice from the entrance of the main lab. That voice was my own.

Both Herbert and von Kriest turned in surprise to see me standing there wearing the uniform of a Prussian security officer and pointing a Luger at them. The large stain of blood covering the white-lined black iron cross pattée emblem proudly adorned the outfit's upper sleeve. That, along with the German model of the firearm I wielded, made it clear that this was a garment taken from one of those pathetic guards von Kriest hired to keep this covert locale secure.

"Dorian," the doctor quietly greeted me with undertones of trepidation.

"Herbert," I responded in the same tone. "I am so pleased to see you again."

"How did…?" was the obvious question the dead Prussian bloke began to ask.

"Did I get past those inept security choices of yours?" I completed it for him. "I wish I could say it was difficult work, but why lie to an honored officer of the Prussian armed forces, even if he happens to be dead? Let us just say that the guard I 'borrowed' this outfit from was as poor a kisser as he was a security officer. He would have been the laughingstock of those splendid Weimar nightclubs I have visited, so all the better that I put him out of his misery. He truly did not expect what he got shoved up his most favored orifice instead of what I promised him." I patted the short sword that was sheathed to my belt for emphasis.

"As for the other two… well, putting on this uniform fooled them for just long enough that they would now be considered a good provider of parts for our mutual friend the doctor to work with if he was fated to remain as your guest."

DORIAN GRAY VS. REANIMATOR
From a Dead Soldier
Christofer Nigro

"Wait…" von Kriest said, boldly taking a step closer to me while fixing his glance on my features. "I recognize you. I will swear to Wotan that we met before. The feeling that we had a prior acquaintance is *very strong,* but I cannot quite place it."

I could tell that the soldier was serious, not just trying to distract me to buy himself time to think of a way out of this predicament. So, I returned his scrutiny.

"Have we met, now? Your rather unpleasant looks mark you as someone I would most certainly not have soiled my hands, mouth, or other treasured parts upon had we met in one of Berlin's finest clubs." Just then my close counter-scrutinization paid off. "Yes! Of course! I saw you on the battlefield during the war a few years ago. You were the last of West's 'reanimates' that I tangled with before the Zepplin dropped the bomb. It seems you escaped being blown to smithereens, much as I did.

"But… you were dead! That is, the walking and killing type of dead that Herbert is fond of creating, but without their characteristic madness of the mind. How is it that you are speaking to me and being in charge of this operation, let alone anything that does not involve biting or bellowing?"

"Now I recognize you also!" von Kriest shouted as he too reached a full recollection "My mind was indeed 'absent' at the time, and I remember little of my first few hours after being given new life from the doctor's reagent. Otherwise, my post-mortem memories start only after absorbing the fumes from Vaast's vials."

So, that's what happened to the good saint's stash. This bastard has so much to answer for. But I must confess that the restoration of his full agency by Vaast's version of the reagent has intrigued me as much as it doubtlessly has Herbert. Perhaps that fluid, or variations of it, may be useful for more than creating nightmares after all.

DORIAN GRAY VS. REANIMATOR
From a Dead Soldier
Christofer Nigro

"I may well owe you something for the circumstances that restored my mind to me after my revival, *Herr*... Dorian, did the doctor call you?" von Kriest said as he attempted to work his persuasive magnetism on me. Unfortunately, he attempted it upon a veritable master of the art of verbal manipulation, and you know what they say about con artists being immune to each other's rhetorical games.

"That would be Dorian *Gray,*" I boasted a bit too proudly. "I cannot in all honesty say it is good to see you again as it is Herbert, if for only purely circumstantial reasons, von Kriest. Yes, I picked up your name while listening in for the last half hour, learning as much of this situation as possible. A face like yours is not one any would be pleased to see in this lifetime, and going through Herbert's reanimation process provides no improvements in that department."

von Kriest gritted his yellow teeth, trying to maintain his temper while dealing with an armed intruder, particularly one who was pointing a gun and had already proven to be a person that one should not be swift to trifle with. He wanted to know who he was facing, to search and probe for any sign of weakness that he could use to secure a deal with me, albeit one that favored only him. Of course, had he already known me well, he would now be taking notes rather than trying to work those tactics.

"Rather than insulting me, Herr Gray," he stated, "let us spend these moments more productively by working out an agreement to our mutual benefit. Let me start by assuring you that Doctor West was taken from where his head was kept for good reason, and I wish to apologize to you if the aristocrat killed by my men in the process was a relative or, erm, paramour of yours."

"Actually, the person your men riddled with lead was not a relative or lover, but *me*. That being the case, what would you guess are the odds that I am remotely desirous of working out any sort of deal with you?"

DORIAN GRAY VS. REANIMATOR
From a Dead Soldier
Christofer Nigro

The look on the soldier's swarthy pale face was indicative of one your sister may have if she accidentally stepped on a dead rat. "Say what, now? Are you too a recipient of West's formulation of the reagent? That does not seem possible, for you show no signs of…"

"You mean, of the mindless homicidal madness," I interjected, "like you initially did, as does virtually all who are unlucky enough to get Herbert's current form of revival treatment? That is most assuredly not the case."

"Did you find one of Vaast's vials before I did?"

"No, sir, as you and your fellow krauts botched my chances for that. But I have no need for such a crude method of restoration. Let us just say that Herbert's methods are not the only ones available and leave it at that. I want no deals with you, and since I grew rather fond of killing your lot during the war, I would much prefer returning you to the abyss that Herbert pulled you back from."

As von Kriest pondered his next attempt at Machiavellian verbiage to save his freakish semblance of life, I realized too late that our brief engagement with each other had resulted in Herbert having the opportunity to put another of his plans in operation. One aspect of his work that von Kriest may have been unaware of was the doctor's use of some sort of lobotomization that enabled him to gain a limited, unstable measure of verbal control over those reanimates of his for the short run.

The temporary body given to Herbert courtesy of a sacrificed superior officer and surgeon seemed unsteady on its knees, but he managed to surreptitiously back away towards the door leading to his specimen storage lab. He would have likely preferred to make this move at a somewhat later point, but he realized that circumstances dictated that the time for action must be now.

He clapped his hands together as a subliminal command to "activate" a half dozen of his reanimates situated in the adjoining specimen lab. They stood up from the surgical tables they laid upon, no longer playing possum. Herbert certainly planned this well, and not surprisingly he did so under the nose of von Kriest.

The undead six charged into the main lab howling like the madmen they now were. The small round burn marks on their foreheads made it clear how Herbert gained this temporary measure of control over them. One of them was dressed in a lab smock similar to the one worn by Herbert himself, and he was likely the earthly remains of the surgeon that grafted the doctor's head to Kimmler's body. Another was a woman, her gray hair still pinned up into a severe bun and dressed in the tattered white linen uniform typically worn by nurses, albeit marred by several ugly stains of blood and bile. There were truly no benefits working for von Kriest, either as a security guard or medical professional.

"It is time to put an end to this farce!" Herbert yelled. "Feel free to fight over me, gentlemen. Just do not expect me to stand around to see how that turns out. Explain any objections you may have over my coming departure with these patients of mine. Gentleman, and lady? Tear those two to pieces!"

"Oh, isn't this just dandy?" I muttered with a glum sigh as I turned my Luger towards three of the advancing cadavers.

"*Gott verdamme dich,* West!" von Kriest cursed at the doctor as he swiftly drew a bayonet strapped to his belt and prepared to defend himself from the three reanimates that targeted him. "You will die painfully after I dispatch these monsters of yours! Painfully and *very slowly!*"

"I doubt you will emerge from this predicament intact enough to do that," Herbert noted as he headed for the main lab's exit.

The good old doctor likely would have escaped if not for the fact that his – or, rather, Kimmler's – legs got extremely wobbly on him after taking a few steps. Herbert cursed as he fell to his knees and struggled to get back up. The necrotic degradation of his temporary body had now evidently reached a critical point, thereby throwing a serious damper on the doctor's intended escape.

"So much for the best laid plans, eh, Herbert?" I quipped to him.

"Shut up, Dorian!" was Herbert's only reply as he placed a now badly trembling hand on a heavy metal table and struggled to pull himself back to his feet.

As the three attacking reanimates converged on me, I fired and struck one of them directly in the forehead, blowing the brains out the back of his skull and ending the fiend's brief return to "life." Before I could fire another bullet, however, the other two running corpses plowed into me, one pushing my arm aside and ruining my next shot. I dropped the firearm as I was pushed against the wall by my two insane antagonists.

The undead maniacs battered and kicked me with psychotic zeal as soon as I was taken to the floor. I blocked my face as best I could, but I knew it would be a short time before one or both leaped on me and attempted to rip out my eyes or bite off my ears… or something equally unpleasant. I would later revive good as new, of course, but this was not an experience that I cared to go through. Furthermore, the interlude would provide Herbert with a chance to escape – as well as a potentially victorious von Kriest getting his hands on me before I had fully healed.

Speaking of von Kriest, he proved himself an apt fighter and every bit as unflinchingly brutal as the trio of mindless brethren that attacked him. His bayonet sliced off the head of his first attacker with a single swipe of the blade. However, the second male cadaver slammed into him while the undead woman bit into his left arm; her fully human teeth tore out a sizable chunk of flesh due to her having lost any trace of the civilized inhibitions she was conditioned with while alive. Or, maybe a part of her mind still recalled what von Kriest did to her when she was a nurse in his employ, and the lady now sought her revenge with due prejudice. I can't be certain if such was true, but I like to think that it was.

He managed to keep hold of his blade during the assault and he slashed at the male corpse that was furiously pummeling him. The murderous cadaver screeched in seeming agony as his belly opened and his bowels spilled out onto the floor. However, this only seemed to enrage the undead bastard further, as he upped the ante of the beating he was so zealously delivering onto his target.

von Kriest's resurrection appeared to have increased whatever resistance to pain he had while fully alive, as he displayed no feelings outside of unbridled rage for combat as his nose was smashed to a pulp and another gob of meat was bitten out of his arm. Instead, he ignored the female's grisly assault on his left arm while he dealt with the much stronger male reanimate that had apparently once been a soldier or security guard. von Kriest thrust the bayonet into the living cadaver's right eye, penetrating the brain and rendering it non-functional once more.

The undead officer next grabbed the eviscerated contents off the floor, wrapping the ropey pink intestines around the throat of the savage female reanimate. He ignored the fact that his left arm had several mouthfuls of flesh chewed out of it as he used the dripping bowel to garrote his foe. The fighting cadaver struggled furiously as her trachea was rapidly crushed, and I can swear that von Kriest appeared to glean a heavy degree of pleasure out of the act.

Thankfully, while this was transpiring, I managed to recover from the serious pummeling I had been taking. I blocked the onslaught of kicks and punches from my two remaining reanimated assailants with my left arm while I reached down and managed to draw my short sword from its sheath. I swiped it back and forth in front of me with all my might and I could see an arm and several fingers belonging to my opponents falling to the floor in bloody heaps. I kicked one of my foes away from me as hard as I could while thrusting my blade into the throat of the other, stifling his insanity-wracked screams and sending him back to the land of the dead.

Despite a missing limb, the final one rushed at me again with a piercing howl that could chill the bones of a grizzly bear. Unfortunately for that chap, his charge afforded him nothing more than a piercing of a different sort, that being my blade into his gut and out the small of his back. This was done less than a minute before von Kriest's aforementioned victory. I took advantage of the meager time allotted me by retrieving my Luger.

I saw that the dropped firearm had slid under a table, and I made haste reaching under it to retrieve the weapon. I noticed that beside the door leading out of the main lab was another that led to a closet converted into a mini-armory, but I could not be certain any gun which may be in there was already loaded. So, I found it a safer bet to reacquire the one I had snatched from the guard during his ill-fated tryst with me.

By this time, Herbert had managed to get back to his feet and he began hobbling towards the door that would provide him egress from the lab. However, that effort was quelled when the strong hand of von Kriest grasped him by the collar of his lab coat and pulled him back into the room. The Prussian *Uhlan* then sliced Herbert's head off Kimmler's now rapidly deteriorating body, and it fell to the floor with a dull thud.

"Oh nooooo…" was all that the mouth of the doctor's perpetually living head could utter in response.

DORIAN GRAY VS. REANIMATOR
From a Dead Soldier
Christofer Nigro

"Oh *yessss,* Doctor!" von Kriest said as he raised his bayonet. "You will pay a most *horrible* price for your treachery, once I deal with Gray!"

"Deal with the coming lead, you misbegotten cunt!" I hollered at the soldier as I pointed the retrieved Luger at him.

Releasing another frenzied shout of rage, von Kriest swiped his bayonet at me in a blindingly fast movement. The blade struck my firearm and sent it flying out of my hand and through the glass of the tenth floor window leading down into the waters of the Thames. And unfortunately, I needed that weapon considerably more than any of the fish in the depths of the river did.

With another quick motion, he swung the blade at my neck, a vicious attempt at decapitation that failed due to my managing to duck underneath it just in time. I then charged at my foe, clutching the wrist of his blade arm while seizing his throat with my other hand.

I made the mistake of thinking that his severely mutilated left arm would not be capable of exerting much force against me. But I saw no sign of that when he utilized the limb to push me several feet back against the wall. With a formidable fury, he struggled to wrest his right hand from my grip and bring the bayonet to bear on me. I then took a chance by releasing his neck and digging my fingers into the deep bite wounds on his left arm. He yelled in response, but I could not tell if this was due to the pain or his ongoing rage, since he did not flinch or loosen his grip. He was quite strong, and I was admittedly unprepared for the level of threat he brought to bear against me.

I was no slouch myself, however, and I quickly drove the fist of my free arm into his diaphragm, using a boxing move I picked up while in Her Majesty's service during the war. von Kriest recoiled just enough for me to send a kick into his solar plexus, forcing him back several feet. He did not go down or crumple from the pain, however; instead, he raised his bayonet to signal the coming of his next attack. But the move did buy me just enough time to draw my short sword.

"Now, kraut, let us see who is the greater master of his respective blade!" I decreed.

"By all means!" von Kriest shouted back. "Have at me, you Tommy mongrel!"

The battle then commenced, and once again I discovered that despite my skill with the blade, von Kriest's was no less able with such a weapon. We countered and parried each other for a few minutes, with each of us eagerly awaiting the other to make a fatal mistake that would allow for the severing of a limb, a thrust through the abdomen, a beheading, or something equally nice.

This resulted in a serious mistake on both our parts. That error was underestimating Herbert, whom we both should have known better than to assume was helpless despite being just a head on the floor. Remember the unusual specimens he had been given to ply his trade on mentioned earlier in this entry? Well, it would turn out that he had done more planning, and more of his sinister work, in the other lab than Van Kriest had anticipated.

Yes, Herbert had a Plan B in case his first choice failed, one that even he was loathe to call into play unless absolutely necessary. But since he did not relish the fate that awaited him regardless of whether it was me or von Kriest that emerged the victor, he felt that he had no choice but to unleash that terrifying back-up plan.

Herbert opened his mouth and shouted the following Latin phrase as loudly as he could: "*Expergiscimini et veni!*"

That call was heard by something in the adjoining specimen lab, a thing which like the six cadavers before it rose from under a cover on a large metal surgical table and trudged into the main lab. Though it was another of Herbert's reanimates, it was quite *unlike* all the others. What ran to the doctor's aid was over seven feet in height, massively muscled, wearing no clothing, and covered almost head to toe with shaggy reddish-brown hair. Or was that fur? Its fully bipedal body was basically human-shaped save for its size and hirsuteness. It had what was obviously a gaping chest wound from a powerful rifle, which revealed how that creature had been killed by someone in the German military.

Could this have been the corpse of one of the elusive and savage wild men that have been a part of European legend since the medieval era? It may once have been, but it now bore a truly disturbing feature (besides being a reanimated carcass) that put it in an entirely different category courtesy of Herbert's ghoulish handiwork.

The wild man's head had been removed and in its place was grafted what I would later learn was the head of Hans Kimmler, the superior officer of von Kriest whom he had murdered in order to provide the doctor with a provisional body. Of course, he would have to make use of the poor wanker's head in such a fashion! The mark in the center of the bald man's brow made it clear that Herbert had lobotomized it, after which he conditioned it to react to that Latin phrase when spoken by his voice.

"Hans… dispatch those two!" the doctor demanded.

The thing's human head turned to look at the two of us battling with its one good eye. I would guess that the thing Kimmler had become retained a primal recollection of his former subordinate officer considering the expression of rage his pale countenance took on when he caught sight of von Kriest. The man's mouth opened and uttered a wailing screech that sounded like a human in both extreme pain and seething anger. With that sentiment expressed, the massive hair-covered body he now controlled charged at us.

von Kriest was so totally focused on achieving a fatal blow against me with his bayonet that he failed to see the Kimmler-headed wild man coming at him. I was certainly not going to give him fair warning, even though for a split second I wondered if it may have been a better idea for the two of us to put our grievances aside for the moment and deal with this threat together. That consideration was quickly taken out of my hands when the Kimmler-thing grabbed von Kriest in its enormous humanlike hands and lifted him into the air as if he weighed no more than a pillow.

"Was ist—?" was all the ruthless soldier had time to utter before the Kimmler wild man tore his body in two with but a modicum of effort. Still living, the upper half of von Kriest shouted and cursed in German, as his arms writhed about in a seeming spasm, before the beast that was once his superior officer hurled him clear through what remained of the windowpane. I could hear the man's rapidly receding scream as his top portion fell ten stories to land in the Thames with a loud splash. von Kriest's body sunk beneath the waves and did not resurface.

The Kimmler wild man then tossed the harmless bottom portion of his first victim's body to the side of the room. I could hear Herbert's throaty laugh as he witnessed one-half of his problem being dealt with in such a viscerally satisfying fashion. I knew I would be next, and I likewise understood that some heavy firepower would give me a much better chance against such a monstrosity than my short sword. So, while von Kriest was being dispatched I ran to the closet armory and kicked the wooden door open.

I knew I had but seconds to find something that was loaded for use, and I did the rare act of sending a thank you to the powers that be in the universe when I saw the partially full spherical fuel tank and hose of a *Wex* flamethrower. This was a truly evil weapon used by the krauts during the war, one I went out of my way not to end up on the receiving end of during my time in the trenches. And that wasn't the only useful item I saw in there. Laying in a dark corner almost obscured beneath a pile of likely unloaded G98 infantry rifles was an absolutely beautiful sight that brought joy to my eyes: a Model 17 *Eierhandgranate* hand grenade.

Going for the flamethrower first, I lifted the nozzle of the *Wex*, opened the valve, and sent a stream of fiery gasoline in the direction of the Kimmler man-beast. That sudden wave of heat caught me unawares (I had never operated one of these things before!) and I only succeeded in setting the floor aflame around the undead creature. The head of the man atop the beast screamed and backed away from the flames. An inferno quickly spread throughout the room as the volatile liquid sprayed all over everything. A wall of fire erupted a short distance from Herbert's sessile but very vocal head. Not one of my better ideas, but I could still see a favorable outcome if I acted properly.

"Dorian!" Herbert shouted. "Get me out of here before the fire reaches me!"

"Worry not, mate!" I yelled back. "As amusing as it would be to watch your head light up like a candle, I need you too much right now. But I'm going to get rid of that abominable thing you created!"

I quickly ran towards the doctor's head and hoisted him up by the shock of hair on his head, not caring in the least if it hurt. I could hear Kimmler's screeches of terror and rage, along with the silhouette of the massive wild man form flaying its mighty arms around, knocking over tables and smashing to bits whatever items of furniture were not yet burning. It was clear that the dreadful beast was trying to find a way through the flames to get its hands on me, and I was not certain that I could outrun such a creature if it succeeded. I was also not keen on allowing such a monstrosity to remain under Herbert's control for however long the effects of the lobotomy might last, and I was now mindful that he could create such dangerous horrors.

Just before dashing out of the room, I ignited the fuse on the grenade and tossed it back through the flames in the general direction of where I could hear Kimmler's frenzied howling. Luckily, I did learn how to use such explosives in the war, and the seconds afforded me before it went off was just long enough to carry Herbert's head along with me as we got safely out of the room. When the explosion went off, I caught a glimpse of the Kimmler wild man being struck by the blast wave and falling through the floor as it collapsed underneath the beast. Several hundred pounds of debris fell down to the next floor on top of the creature, after which its mournful wailing went silent.

I managed to grab a blanket off a table before leaving out the back entrance so I could conceal my bodiless companion's head inside of it. I certainly didn't want to be seen carrying Herbert in his partial condition while I ran down the fog-enshrouded streets alongside the Thames. The last thing I saw before exiting the neighborhood was a tongue of flame burst out the tenth floor window where the lab was located. As I sprinted back towards the West End house I had rented with my mate's severed head in tow I was firmly hoping that the entire building would burn down – along with everything inside of it.

"Consider yourself lucky I have need of you, Herbert," I said to my bodiless companion cloaked inside the blanket I carried. "I understand that it was no fault of yours that von Kriest did such a number on me while kidnapping you, but I will not and cannot forget what you tried to do during my generous rescue attempt."

"And can you truly blame me for that, Dorian?" Herbert replied in a voice slightly muffled within the blanket. "Considering what you are capable of, would you not have done your best in my place to escape from falling into your hands again?"

"Point taken, mate. Nevertheless, I was almost tempted to leave you to smolder in the heat… or in the clutches of that beastly thing you created out of Himmler's and a wild man's parts once you eventually lost control over it. This time, at least, you are being conscripted to use your talents for good."

"Good, Dorian? Had I a body right now, I would shudder at the thought of what may constitute 'good' in your debauched eyes. You have a strong propensity for throwing your share of stones outside the house of glass that your decadent soul dwells within. That is, if you even still have a soul considering the price that may have been exacted from you by whatever forces empower that portrait of yours. Ponder these words of mine the next time you consider lecturing me about what nightmares I may bring into the world."

I did not reply to Herbert about that. I was simply not prepared to concede more than one point to him in a single day.

END

BODY POLITICS

Christofer Nigro

PART I: EMILY DOESN'T LIVE HERE ANYMORE

Dorian Gray's Private Journal. London, Mid-January 1922

I continued walking down the fog-shrouded streets of London after Midnight, thankful that few besides the periodic drunk were out and about. Visibility was also quite poor, so none who had been over-imbibing on the Famous Grouse this evening were likely to see me as anything out of sorts. However, I was fervently aware that among the few whom I may run into this hour was a peeler walking his beat, and those blighters tended to have a keen eye for one who is up to no good. I would know since that is typically me, and I have had more than my share of encounters of the constabulary sort.

It was imperative that I should go unmolested, and the all-important cargo I carried secured within a thick blanket in my arms remain undiscovered, until I reached the old St. Ives Cathedral on the East End. Not because I had any intentions of going to confession at this late hour. Were I to ever do that, I would be there for hours on end detailing my ample number of sins to a voyeuristic priest who likely had an equal number of improprieties to reckon with.

73

DORIAN GRAY VS. REANIMATOR
Body Politics
Christofer Nigro

The two clergymen whom I had simultaneous relations with at St. Vincent's two months ago could readily attest to that. As would a third from that same cathedral, whom I caught secretly helping himself to both the wine supply and the donations from the collection plate. Yes, I happened to take note of quite a few shenanigans during the unholy trysts I enjoyed within that holiest of places.

No, what – or, rather, *whom* – I was carrying beneath the blanket was of the utmost importance. As was the unfortunately similar individual whose place of residence I was then headed towards.

"Dorian!" came the somewhat muffled voice of Dr. Herbert West's head from within the concealing cloth in my arms. "Are we there yet?"

"Dear Lord, Herbert," I replied. "I swear you are worse than an anxious old lady one is apt to find sitting beside them in a shared hansom ride that wishes to make it on time to her knitting club meeting."

"Joke all you like, Dorian, but I am unfortunately at your mercy for the time being, not knowing where we are headed or why you have need of me. And I am getting dust particles and lint in my eyes under this damned blanket!"

"Please do forgive me for the particles, the lint, and my lack of concern for your situation, Herbert. You've been through far worse. As for where we are headed, we will be calling upon a... gentleman whom you have much in common with, and whom it's about time you met. I fear I will need his skills to get you back into a condition capable of lending me aid, and also to help us accomplish a most important task."

"My curiosity is now roundly piqued, Dorian. Who might this exquisitely learned man whom you displayed such hesitation to call a 'gentleman' be?"

DORIAN GRAY VS. REANIMATOR
Body Politics
Christofer Nigro

"I… would prefer not to utter his name aloud outdoors, even in a low tone of voice on the sparsely traversed, post-Witching Hour streets."

"A man who must be spoken of in such a hushed fashion, eh? I am now past being intrigued. But wouldn't this hour of the evening be a bad time to expect anyone to be awake, let alone in the mood to receive company? Especially of the type that you and I represent?"

"Worry not, Herbert. This chap is used to working late hours on his various projects, so as not to interfere with his 'day job,' that being nothing but a cover for his preferred activities. As for not wanting our company, well… let us just say that he owes me a favor or two. He would be naught but ashes now, were it not for a certain timely intervention of mine."

"I see. So, he is one of the many fellows of your acquaintance who would kill you should the opportunity present itself. He sounds like the type of company you would keep, Dorian."

"And yours as well, Herbert. In fact, when you meet him, I daresay you will find that he has much more in common with you than he does with me."

"Really? My curiosity now simmers at a boiling point. When will we arrive at his home? Or perhaps I should reiterate… are we there yet?"

"Oh, do shut up, Herbert. His current residence is now just down the street. I can easily spot the distinct architecture of St. Ives Cathedral even through all this fog."

"St. Ives? Is this man a priest?"

"Certainly not. I would be more elated for his late-night company if such were the case, as men of God tend to be quite fun to sin with. However, the man whom you are only a few minutes from meeting is, like you, a Doctor of Medicine and alchemical brewer of the strange and monstrous sort; a creator of nightmares and a proud violator of the natural order. I wager that based on my description, you like him already, eh, Herbert? And as I said before, your meeting with one of his infamous lineage is long overdue."

"Why does such a man reside in a church, then?"

"He only dwells within its spacious basement area, where he has a laboratory set up. You can ask him how that came to be his current hidden base of operations in just a moment."

I slipped through the space between the iron-spiked gate where I would find the back entrance to the huge Gothic building, careful not to drop Herbert as I did so. But the grunting noise he uttered beneath the blanket made it clear that the tight squeeze with him in my arm was quite painful. I attempted to hide my merriment at his discomfort before speaking again.

"Sorry, Herbert."

"I doubt it, Dorian."

As I moved to the worn oakwood door marking the back entrance that led into the cellar, a section of the building that almost no one ever treads, I proceeded to pound on the door several times.

"Victor, I know you're down there, fully awake and feverishly at work on your latest horrific experiment. But I have need of you this evening, after which the remainder of your debt will be partially squared. I also have someone with me – or, at least a part of him thereof – that I believe you should really meet."

After a moment I could hear the church's secret resident rushing up the stone steps leading to the door. He opened it, and it was no surprise to me that despite the grueling and often messy work he was conducting, the bloke was nevertheless immaculately dressed. Only the fact that his sleeves were rolled up would indicate that he was conducting a task in a basement medical lab rather than out on a soiree to the finest London theater.

DORIAN GRAY VS. REANIMATOR
Body Politics
Christofer Nigro

"Dorian Gray, as I live and breathe!" my quasi-friend said upon opening the door to look upon my fair, forever youthful visage.

"Yes, it is good to see that you currently *are* among the living and breathing, Baron! For I have need of you this night. May I enter your holy domain?"

"I suppose I am obliged to grant you entrance," he replied with strained courtesy. "But do hurry up, as I would prefer not taking the chance that any of the staff may see me admitting a guest."

As I shut the door behind me and descended the hard, cold stairs behind our host, his regal countenance suddenly took on a confounded expression. "Wait, did you not say that you had someone with you that I should meet?"

"Oh, yes! Wherever are my manners?" I opened the blanket to reveal the disembodied but still quite animate head of Dr. Herbert West.

My host's eyes displayed but a mild expression of surprise upon the sight before him. For one such as he, what he now beheld was nothing beyond the pale.

"Dr. Herbert West," I said, "allow me to introduce you to our esteemed host… Baron Victor Frankenstein."

***

"Herbert West…" the Baron said with a smile now adorning his imperial features. "Testimony regarding your work has most certainly reached my part of the world. This is an honor, even though I must express condolences as to your current condition."

"Baron Frankenstein…" Herbert lamented with a degree of reverential awe which equaled the amount expressed by our host. "I, like some others in my circle, had always suspected that the events depicted in Shelley's novel, the stage productions based on it, and in that Edison film a few years back were describing a real event and a real lineage with your name. After all, Dorian's story was likewise recorded by an author though presented to the public as a work of fiction. But to see you still… living, and apparently in good health after more than a century following those events…"

"For one thing," Victor interjected, "the quest to unravel the secrets of life extension are not unique to you alone, my friend. More of my lineage besides myself have found a means of doing so; though in my case, it is a rather complicated affair. Perhaps one day I shall have the time to tell you the tale in full.

"Secondly, but of course the story connected to the various lines of my family name is authentic. However, the proper term would be *stories*, as in the plural. The events recorded in that novel were taken from notes dictated to a sea captain… and the Victor Frankenstein who did so, and perished soon afterwards, was my grandfather. Others in our clan inherited his scientific genius and his admirable determination to conquer and circumvent death.

"One of these others was the subject of that film, though Edison presented it to the public as a fictional 'adaptation' of Shelley's novel. Perhaps one day your story will likewise be the subject of 'gothic' fiction in the hands of one of those authors with an uncanny knack for uncovering the secret history of the world."

"Actually," Herbert stated, "before the sequence of events that landed me in my present condition began, I was contacted by some eccentric but undeniably brilliant writer by the name of Lovecraft. This author had become privy to documents concerning my work and managed to contact and interview my former assistant Daniel Cain. So, he requested confirmation of some of the more 'fantastic' elements of my work according to that conference. He also said he would 'cover' for me by presenting my anecdotes to the public as a work of fiction. I found that prospect amusing, so I exchanged a few letters with him. I am not certain anything will come of the info I shared as it did with you and Dorian, however."

"I must say, Herbert, what a delightfully uncanny name that writer acquaintance of yours has," I said. "By all means, give him full access to your story once you regain the ability to utilize a typewriter. I delight in how such authors bring the names of our ilk to public attention while convincing them we are only products of fiction. Hence, we may revel in the infamy acquired while simultaneously avoiding the actual scrutiny of the masses... even if it may, at times, present something of an inconvenience to hiding our true identities. Then again, most of those whom I have shared my real name with never once considered that I could possibly be the actual man in the book."

"Yes, yes, I know how the human psychological phenomenon of rationalization works, Dorian," Victor retorted. "People need to believe they live in an ordered world whose worst terrors and threats outside of a battlefield are only products of the imagination. That enables the likes of us to go about our work quietly despite achieving a form of celebrity status."

Herbert's eyes then moved around to take in as much of the spacious expanse of the cathedral's lowest level as they could without having the benefit of a neck to turn his head around. "This is an impressive setup you have here, Baron," he noted. "How did you ever happen to secure this arrangement with the church? Considering, well, how the work you do here would seem to those of the Catholic mindset to usurp the authority of their God?"

The Baron was quick to explain. "The clergy who tenant St. Ives, like many of their ilk, tend to be as lax in devotion to any set of principles as the people who attend their mass to receive moral lectures about a God who allows them and their loved ones to die. So, when I discovered this place and decided its cavernous basement would be perfect for me, I attended services there to become acquainted with its pastor. I then began secretly following him during his evening sojourns to 'save the souls' of the more sinful residents of London by bringing the Eucharist to them.

"I soon learned that during his visits to a certain 'house' on Aberdeen Street, he was giving the ladies employed there quite a bit more than Eucharistic wafers to consume. You see, rather than venturing to that 'den of iniquity' to save the souls of the employees by spreading the word of God to them as he claimed, he was in actuality using them to rescue *him* from his vow of celibacy. Moreover, what he was giving to the bad seeds there was nothing more than some seed of his own, all paid for by the coin in the church's donation platter."

"Ha!" I reacted. "I am quite fond of Madam Cossette's place myself. The variety of services it offers is delightful; I dare say those ladies are willing to do *anything*. Ha! Ha! I can hardly blame the pastor for 'giving unto temptation' while making his soul-saving rounds there."

Herbert took on an expression suggesting that he would have shaken his head if he still had a neck.

"Nevertheless," I continued, "it is quite fortuitous that you were able to work out a deal, if such is what you would call it, with the pastor for this great space beneath the cathedral, Victor."

"Yes, quite," the Baron concurred. "Father Pence was very amenable with working out the details of offering me a covert residency and workspace down here. As well as generously allocating a share of the church donations to help finance the moving of my lab equipment to the basement surreptitiously."

"What a truly magnanimous sort the pastor of this church must be!" I decreed with a grin. "I should start attending masses here myself. And I surely would if I weren't already quite satisfied with the services offered by the clergy at St. Vincent's. But perhaps I shall have the chance to make the acquaintance of this Father Pence should I ever happen to run into him at the bordello."

Eager to change the subject, Herbert said, "This is not my main point of interest with the Baron here." His eyes shifted to Victor. "Baron, did you not mention others in your family tree being involved in similar activities to your grandfather, with their chroniclers tending to conflate all of them as 'adaptations' of the single incident recorded by Shelly?"

"Yes," the Baron confirmed. "What makes that task easier is how popular the name 'Victor' happens to be for males as either a first or middle name throughout the various lines of my lineage, along with other names such as 'Henry.' These choices are to honor those in a heritage that extends back to the Franks that once conquered the land of Gaul on this continent.

"For instance, one of my family to follow in the esteemed footsteps of my genealogy besides myself was my uncle Aloysius, who like another uncle of mine named Henry, was a student of Dr. Septimus Pretorius – whose name and career you may also be familiar with – and they earned their medical degrees partly under his tutelage. No author of esoteric means has yet to record either of their stories as an 'adaptation' of my grandfather's ill-fated saga in any type of medium... but give it time.

"Yet the most interesting thing about my Uncle Aloy, at least as far as you are concerned, Dr. West, is that he is likewise here in my basement sanctuary, albeit unbeknownst to that of the cathedral staff."

"He is?" Herbert queried with elated surprise. "Where is he? How have you managed to hide him here? May I meet him as well?"

"I will gladly answer all three of those questions immediately," Victor responded with one of those genial yet unsettling smiles of his. "After all, my good doctor, you will see that Uncle Aloy currently has much more in common with you than I do myself."

He then sauntered over to one of the several wooden tables decorating the capacious basement deep beneath St. Ives. On it was what appeared to be a large square box-shaped object of wide circumference covered by a sheet. The Baron pulled the cover off to reveal a most astounding sight: a glass tank filled with some type of viscous yet fully transparent fluid, within which was the disembodied head of a relatively young man with brown hair and a thin mustache.

The head was affixed to some sort of platform located at the bottom of the enclosure. A few wires had been surgically connected to various points on his facial skin and extended out of the tank to some of the lab machinery. That aforementioned skin was covered in small stiches and sutures that appeared to be an attempt to repair severe damage to the epidermis. The decapitated chap's eyes were closed, and he showed no sign of movement or cogency.

"Now isn't that interesting in the most ironic of ways," I quietly noted aloud. "It would seem you are less unique in this world than you may have thought, Herbert."

The Baron simply smiled again and said, "Dr. West... Dorian... meet Aloysius Victor Henry Frankenstein. Yes, he was given *two* middle names to honor the familial popularity of both, as his elite parents were unable to resolve their argument as to which of the two he should be christened with. He has been addressed as both interchangeably throughout his life... one that has turned out to be much longer, and considerably less pleasant, than he had expected."

"How... did *he* end up like this?" Herbert asked.

"Simple," was Victor's reply. "Similar to myself, Aloy followed the family's scientific tradition and created new individuals from the cast-off refuse of spent lives. He then utilized a combination of arcane chemicals and the harnessing of galvanic energies to give it life and consciousness, and… well, history tends to repeat itself, particularly for those in my lineage. It is almost as if we are cursed to endlessly repeat the errors of our predecessors.

"More specifically, Aloysius died after he and his Monster pursued each other in the Siberian badlands, but unlike the original flesh golem created by my grandfather, the regrets felt by this one towards the death of his father did not take the form of solemn remorse. Rather, they centered on disappointment that a natural demise from exposure, starvation, and exhaustion had robbed him of revenge on his sire. So, utilizing the techniques he had learned from his creator, the Monster carried Aloy's corpse back to the lab and intimidated his assistant into aiding the creature in bringing him back to life in a body that would never die. That way, he would be forced to suffer eternally in the same fashion that his creation did.

"To make a long story shorter, Aloy escaped the lab to run afoul of irate villagers who tore him to pieces – I can most certainly relate to that – but the galvanically charged bits of his body did not die. His still conscious head fell into the non-tender clutches of his former teacher, Pretorius, and through a complex series of events it later ended up falling into my care."

"So that, like me, your Uncle Aloy is now a living head?" Herbert queried. "And you are endeavoring to keep it in fully functional condition?"

"But of course," Victor replied. "What I may learn from him is too important to honor his repeated requests to utilize my expertise in finding a means of killing him. As a fellow scientist, one would think he should understand my decision."

"As usual, all brains and no heart, Victor," I bantered. "You and Herbert truly are a match made in Heaven. Or would that be Hell? And he and your uncle make a different sort of match. Ha! Ha!"

"Mind your manners, Dorian," Victor retorted. "The pursuit of scientific progress could be a boon to the entire human species. The good of one or two souls among the multitude cannot outweigh the potential benefits to all mankind. Is that not correct, Dr. West?"

"I can understand your point, Baron," was Herbert's predictable reply. "I too have had to make such judgment calls. Erring on the side of progress and knowledge is, I must say, the lesser of certain evils."

I rolled my eyes. *Keep believing that, gentlemen. That's why I love you two so much.*

"But… is Aloy's head catatonic?" was Herbert's next query.

"Oh, not at all," Victor answered. "He simply finds his situation so traumatic that he prefers to sleep off the misery, so to speak. But I must confess that ignoring my guests, particularly one of your esteem, is unforgivably rude. I will see to rectifying that."

The Baron walked to the table where the tank was situated, picked up a metal measuring stick, and loudly smacked it against the glass a few times. This caused poor Aloysius's head to start back into full consciousness. His eyes abruptly opened, revealing a soft blue color which strangely mirrored that of Herbert's own. The mouth also gaped wide and let out a sound resembling a combination gasp and scream.

Whatever the nature of the fluid the head was immersed in, it proved able to carry sound better than ordinary water. Hence, the man's voice and words were fully

84

comprehensible to human ears outside the tank, with the only hindrance being that they sounded as if they were spoken through a mask of cloth.

"Dear God, what are you doing to me now, Victor?" Aloysious's head shouted.

The Baron simply smiled yet again. "No need for the drama, Uncle Aloy. I want you to meet Dr. Herbert West, an eminent scientific brain pursuing ends similar enough to ours. As you can see, he is presently suffering a… condition not unlike your own."

Aloy's frenzied eyes turned to meet Herbert's, which was situated on a table just across from his.

"Greetings, Aloysious," my similarly bodiless friend said with a good sense of graciousness. "It is quite an honor to meet a second member of the Frankenstein clan mere minutes after being introduced to the first I have ever met."

"Did Victor do this to you?" was Aloy's only response.

"No, no, he did not," Herbert clarified. "My predicament came about from an entirely unrelated source. And in fact, your nephew is going to help me get back on two feet of my own, to coin a phrase."

"You fool!" Aloy cried in return. "Victor never helps anyone but himself! Please kill me! And then kill Victor! Before he does something worse than this to you, or to some other poor soul! Please, I am begging you!"

"Victor, you seem to be as popular with your family as I am with my own," I stated with a snigger.

The Baron tossed me a sour look before scampering over to some small device to which one of the wires embedded in his uncle's facial skin was connected to.

"Aloys, this uncalled-for behavior only serves to compound your earlier rudeness, so I think you should go back to sleep now," Victor declared.

He then pushed a button on the mechanism that sent a potent electrical shock down through the wire and into

Aloy's submerged head. The disembodied scientist's facial muscles contorted horribly, and his eyes bulged to the point that I thought they would be ejected from their sockets. The lids and the mouth then closed, and all was back to silence save for the gentle hum of the device feeding power to the tank. Victor then threw the tarpaulin over the tank again to conceal its contents.

"Forgive me, Dr. West," the Baron said. "I regretfully confess that not all members of my family possess my sense of etiquette to work in tandem with their scientific mind. I fear that unlike you, Aloy's condition has made him delusional, so he is prone to irrational outbursts. That is why I prefer to let him sleep whenever possible."

Upon hearing that, I scoffed and smirked at the same time.

"I see," was Herbert's verbal reaction. "Which leads to the next of my questions, Baron. Why have you yet to find your uncle a body to replace the one he lost like you say you are going to do for me?"

"Trust me, I have my reasons, good sir," Victor responded. "But rather than burden you with irrelevant information, I would like to get down with the business at hand. I am a busy man, you know."

"Of course," Herbert concurred with the Baron, eager to get on with things himself. "Which actually leads to another of my questions for you: Where are you going to get a suitable body for me?"

"That is an easy question to answer," Victor cordially replied, "as I always keep such an inventory here."

Victor then managed to startle even me by walking to the far end of the cavernous cathedral basement and pulling a rope to retract a curtain covering a row of large glass containers. Each of them held the sessile nude bodies of male cadavers, all of which looked fully intact and in pristine shape. I was put at great unease since it reminded me of such

86

supplies from another extraordinary individual I had recently crossed swords with and had almost lost my immortal life to (that one operating in similar secrecy, albeit in the back of a men's clothing store).

Herbert's countenance beamed with satisfaction at the sight. Victor was indeed capable of providing the parts required, as well as the expertise to affix my ersatz friend's head to one of them.

***

"You will feel a biting sting for just a few seconds, Dr. West," Victor informed my beheaded friend as he injected a potent sedative into the left side of his face.

"I assure you I have felt far worse than a mere needle in my day, Baron," he replied.

"I can attest to that," I added, "as I used a much bigger pointed object to slice off his head."

Victor shrugged off my comment while making the injection. "You should sleep through the entire procedure, my good sir. It will be most delicate work attaching the nerves of your head to your donor body so that they perfectly synch as one organism when charged by the energies of my galvanic generators, so I want to take my time with it.

"There, now. you should fall into a peaceful slumber within a minute; and when you awaken, you shall be a whole being again."

"Many thanks, Dr. Frankenstein," Herbert replied just before the drugs took effect. "I will owe you much after…"

All was then quiet on the operating table. I watched the ghastly but fascinating actions of Baron Victor Frankenstein with great interest and assisted the Baron now and then the best that one without any professional medical training possibly could.

***

Herbert's eyes opened several hours later.

"Welcome back, sleepy head," I quipped with a smile.

My less-than-good friend's initially blurry vision rapidly cleared to see Victor walking over to him. "How are you feeling, Dr. West? Everything went well. The nerves are perfectly attached, your new body is sufficiently charged, and its retained muscle memory should enable you to move and walk without obstruction in less than an hour."

"I... feel rather strange," Herbert said as he lifted the arm of his newly attached body and looked at the rugged hands taken from a sculptor.

"That is quite normal following such a procedure," the Baron assured him. "This body is not your own, and the joined nervous systems will take a brief period of adjustment as they fully mesh together. Nevertheless, the potent voltaic charge should make them synchronize to an enormous extent."

"I do understand..." Herbert uttered in a state of relative calm... that is, until he raised the limb further to find that it possessed a powerful but misshapen musculature and was covered in shaggy tufts of hair.

"What... in the name... of...?" was my friend's not-very-happy reaction as he laid eyes on that grotesque appendage that was now his.

He was even more stunned and irate when he sat up and looked down to behold exactly what type of body his head had been enjoined to. It was one that resembled a hirsute Neanderthal, greatly muscled and looking as much simian as human. In fact, it was not too unlike a previous chimeric patchwork body he once created, a wild man apparently shot to death by a German soldier somewhere in the Black Forest, to which he had grafted the head of a certain Prussian

Oberleutnant onto. This one, however, had a much thinner covering of hair and was not nearly as towering in height.

Herbert leapt off the metal table a bit awkwardly, but with a surprising degree of agility, nonetheless. He quickly demonstrated the prodigious strength of this new body by knocking over the operating slab with a single swipe of his burly arm. It was clear that the normal human hands attached to this form did not belong to its original owner.

"What is the meaning of this, Frankenstein?" Herbert demanded to know as he scampered over to the Baron in a most aggressive fashion, in which he resembled an ape moving about in a fully bipedal manner. "You led me to believe you would attach me to one of those perfect athletic bodies stored in those glass cylinders of yours!"

"Why, I did nothing of the sort, Dr. West," Victor responded, cautiously backing away from the now massively strong Herbert West but still holding a firm composure. After all, staring into the face of monstrous beings brought back from the dead was nothing new to the Baron. "I merely used them as a frame of reference when I mentioned how I always keep a ready supply of bodies around. I never said I would give you one of the few perfect specimens in my possession. It was agreed that this was merely intended as a temporary body, so as to allow you to work on the personal project that our mutual friend has yet to reveal to us. So, why waste the best specimens at my disposal for that?"

"Frankenstein, this was a flagrant deception on your part, and you know it!" Herbert exclaimed as he took another sudden step towards the Baron. "Do not take me for a fool! You are dealing with an equal here, not the usual rabble you consort with and manipulate to your own ends with impunity! It would seem that your unfortunate uncle's warning was in no way delusional, as you claimed!"

"Dr. West, I must ask you to calm yourself and step back," Victor said firmly. "I am not one to be trifled with even on my worst day. And I assure you this is *not* one of my worst days."

"We shall see, Frankenstein..."

That was when I stepped between them. I had to douse the flame that was igniting in my presence before it erupted into a raging inferno. I needed these two, and that meant I could not afford to have them at each other's throats. At least, not at this time.

"Now, now, gentlemen," I said, "let us maintain some semblance of decorum and civility here. We shall all have plenty of time in the future to try and kill each other. But for now, we have a task before us that requires each of us to remain intact. Or, at least comparatively speaking, in Herbert's case."

The scientists seemed to calm down a bit, but they remained staring balefully in each other's eyes, the way two male cats typically do when confronting each other. Further intercession on my part was clearly warranted.

"Herbert, as the Baron said, this is but a temporary body. Just so you are mobile enough to perform the required task at hand. We shall work on finding the pieces of your original body once you complete the favor required of you. Is that satisfactory?"

Herbert's real teeth clenched along with hands that were not his own but nevertheless now controlled by his nervous system. Victor stood looking impassively forward, displaying only a modicum of fear along with a heap of preparedness for whatever happened to come his way during the next few unpredictable moments.

"Very well," Herbert said while taking a few steps back, nearly tripping over the large, spade-like feet he was just becoming used to. "But I would refrain from any further treachery, Frankenstein. Let us do what we must for Dorian... and then part the ways."

DORIAN GRAY VS. REANIMATOR
Body Politics
Christofer Nigro

"Agreed," Victor replied with just a hint of acid in his voice.

"But tell me," Herbert continued, "who – or *what* – did this body belong to?"

"That would be Herr Schnieder, one of the patients under my care at the sanitarium where I worked as the lead psychiatrist many years back."

"In your 'care?'" I scoffed with a smirk. "Then it is no surprise to me that things did not turn out well for the poor bastard. Did *any* of the patients under your tender ministrations survive your tenure there?"

"Mind the sarcasm in my house, Dorian!" Victor growled.

"Tell me more about this 'Herr Schnieder,' Baron," Herbert requested while looking at his grotesque new body in a wall mirror with a revolted expression on his face. "I should know exactly what I am joined with for the immediate future."

Victor obliged the request. "As I was explaining before Dorian's juvenile interruption, Schnieder was a patient of mine while I worked at a sanitarium. And a most unusual patient, at that. He was evidently born an atavistic throwback to humanity's more primal past when our ancient ancestors were more beast than man. Much as I suspect those wild men from various reports coming in from the forests of England and elsewhere may constitute a rare breeding population of the same.

"I envy your being able to work on such a specimen in the recent past, Dr. West. Herr Schnieder was the closest I have come to being able to examine and work my expertise on such a being thus far.

"As you have discovered, he was – *is* – quite strong, and he used that strength to break out of confinement and commit suicide. I brought him back to life and gave him the brains of a brilliant doctor and the hands of an expert sculptor. But

91

the being he became proved even more difficult to control than the one he had been, and the rest of the patients assaulted and killed him again by ripping out his viscera. I had to carefully scrape them off the floor and stitch them back into his abdomen as best I could. That, alas, is why you may suffer from a degree of abdominal discomfort and bowel trouble while you remain connected to that body. My apologies ahead of time for that likely unpleasantness."

Herbert looked down at the huge surgical scar on the pronounced paunch of the troglodyte body he was now joined with. He also winced upon hearing Victor's faux *mea culpa* and condolences.

I covered my face to muffle a sudden spurt of laughter. "It was thoughtful of you to warn Herbert about that before proceeding with the surgery, Victor," I said. "Oh, wait, you didn't; you waited until *now* to do so."

Victor ignored my acerbity and completed his narration on the original owner of Herbert's new body. "So, I then placed Schnieder's repaired body into cryo-stasis until such time as I should ever need it again. One never knows when such a circumstance may present itself, as your visit here today has made abundantly clear."

"What an ironic day this is for our mutual friend," I remarked with a snigger. "Not only did he happen to meet another disembodied head, but he again found himself confronted with a human head sutured to the form of a hairy beast-man. Only in this particular instance, the head was his own."

"Dorian… what exactly do you need us for?" Herbert enquired with an exasperated tone as he shifted the subject to the exact matter at hand.

"That, Herbert, will bring yet another example of irony into this basement," I replied. "But first, I must get *her* transported over here. Victor, is there a phone in this place?"

DORIAN GRAY VS. REANIMATOR
Body Politics
Christofer Nigro

"Yes, unfortunately, there is," he said while pointing to the stick telephone sequestered on a small table in a dark corner of the spacious cellar. "I never use those infernal things, as I fail to understand why anyone would choose such a means of communication over an in-person conversation. You learn so much by speaking to people face-to-face and observing both their expressions and the immediate environment which they speak in. Hence, I shall never understand the popularity of such a device. One day I wager some fool will invent a mobile version that people can carry about with them much as they now do a purse."

"Ha! I very much doubt it will ever go that far," I opined. "After all, not even Edison or Tesla themselves could ever make a wire long enough for a phone that one carried wherever they went. But please do give me a moment to dial a request to one of my other contacts."

After selecting the proper numbers in the rotary, the phone rang but twice before it was picked up. "Many thanks and more thanks for waiting at the house until you received this call, David," I said to the personage on the other line. "That is another one I owe you. Now that it's evening, you should be able to safely bring the hatbox here. Just be careful with it, do you understand? '[...]' That is *not* amusing, David. Just bring the box to the address I gave you, and I shall see you shortly. Goodbye."

"Do I ever hate vampires sometimes," I griped while replacing the receiver on the phone. "But they do have their uses. Once my acquaintance David arrives with her, I shall reveal what I need the pair of you for. Be prepared for another shock, my dear Herbert, as you shall soon become re-acquainted with someone whom I am certain you hoped that you would never see again."

***

93

DORIAN GRAY VS. REANIMATOR
Body Politics
Christofer Nigro

"If that… deliveryman of yours will soon be arriving with some lady you mentioned," Victor said, "should you not leave to meet him at the corner of Aberdeen now?"

"Oh, there is no need for that," I told him. "David is going to come right to the door here."

Victor became incensed at the news. "You gave him the address to the church itself rather than merely telling him to meet you at the corner of this street? And this vampire – I am presuming he is an *actual* member of the Undead, and not another poser for effect or cannibalistic murderer described as such – was made privy to my hidden laboratory in this basement?"

"David is a trusted confidante, and he owes me a few favors," I replied, trying to calm Victor, as he could be unpredictably dangerous when his temper flared. The good Baron's notorious madness always varies in its degree, and I try to keep it to a modicum during my dealings with him. "If you can trust *me* with your secret, you can trust him as if he were an extension of me."

"And you believe Dorian's claim that vampires are real, Baron?" was Herbert's query. "I mean, a man of science and rationality like yourself?"

"I do indeed," Frankenstein affirmed. "For I have met a few in the past. And do we not both accept the reality of Dorian's apparently supernatural source of immortality, connected as it is to a portrait? Furthermore, would many not find the work we do, the resurrection of the dead, as unbelievable and beyond reality as anything akin to a vampire?

"When you consider that, it should become easier for men like us to accept the reality of such creatures, perhaps owing their existence to some aspect of science that has yet to be cataloged and mastered by the conventional scientific establishment."

DORIAN GRAY VS. REANIMATOR
Body Politics
Christofer Nigro

"Point taken," Herbert acquiesced. "But now I find myself anxious over this mysterious lady that Dorian's courier is bringing here as if she was unable to travel herself…" That is when the realization hit him. "Wait, I recall you mentioning a hatbox to this David person on the telephone. You couldn't possibly mean…?"

That is when we heard a loud knocking on the door. My messenger had arrived.

"Victor," I said, "I believe you will have to invite David in so that he will be able to enter with his delivery."

"Ah, yes, of course," my host noted. "But know that I will be keeping a wary eye on him, and that I am familiar with the means of dispatching one of his kind if necessary."

"Worry not, his visit shall be brief," I reassured my partner-in-machinations.

Victor opened the door to behold an eccentric but oddly attractive man with flaxen hair and clown makeup covering his face. His garb was otherwise reminiscent of those gangsters then running rampant across the American metropolis known as Chicago: a dark tuxedo with red pinstripes, a gray necktie, a red top visible underneath, a dark fedora with a similarly red band encircling above the brim, and black spatter dash shoes that looked as if they had cost a pristine penny.

The visitor's hands appeared to be as chalk white as the grease paint adorning his face, a comical yet slightly sinister look completed by black fingernails. In his right hand was a most unusual black cane, as it ended in a small white skull of unknown substance rather than a typical knob of wood. In his other arm was the all-important hatbox.

"Hey there, handsome!" David said to Victor. "I'm guessing you're the owner of this 'chamber of horrors,' as Dorian called it?"

"David, do put a leash on your mouth," I said in an irritated tone.

DORIAN GRAY VS. REANIMATOR
Body Politics
Christofer Nigro

"But if I did that, then I couldn't bite anyone," he rebutted. "Or regale anyone with my charming spiel." He then turned back to Victor. "So, stud, may I come in? Or are you going to let me stand out here in this freezing foggy night?"

"Do not be dramatic, David," I commented, "as you know the cold doesn't affect you."

"Yeah, I know, but it's just the principle of the matter," he blathered with his characteristic half-smirk.

"Do come in," Victor said with a stiff tone, giving David the required invitation to get his visit over and done with.

"Wow, lookit this place!" the vampiric clown noted as he stepped into the basement and beheld Victor's impressive display of equipment. "It looks like science goes on here! Probably the type that would give all decent people nightmares! Ha! I love it!"

The Baron scoffed. Herbert looked on with an expression of intrigue.

"Don't worry, my regal sir," David said in response to Victor's reaction. "I'm not a decent person, so I completely approve of this place! I need to get a set-up like this for an exhibit at my carnival! And by the way, though I didn't catch your first name, is your last name by any chance 'Frankenstein?' And if it is, chances are your first name will be either 'Victor' or 'Henry,' am I right? And if not, your middle name will be one or the other, huh?"

Now the Baron was completely taken aback. "How would you know that? Did Dorian reveal that sensitive information to you?"

"Oh no, not our Dorian!" David reassured the Baron. "He wouldn't rat out something like that if I didn't absolutely need to know it. You just look like a Frankenstein. I've met a few of your clan before, and the family resemblance is unmistakable. Your stately profile and haughty demeanor all but gave it away on their own. But this lab of yours was the

96

kicker since only a Frankenstein would put something like *this* together."

David began looking around. "Hey, is that a galvanic generator over there? And where do you keep the bodies? C'mon, you wouldn't be worthy of the name Frankenstein if you didn't have corpses stashed around someplace for your twisted experiments. Can I watch your next one? I've always wanted to see a brain transplant! Heh!"

Before Victor could utter a response that we may all have regretted, I made a point to step in. "David, can you please hand me the hatbox and go lose yourself in the fog outside? Thank you for a job well done but know that the job *is* done."

"Urg, you're not your usual fun self tonight, Dorian," David grumbled as he handed me the box. "This is it, right? You said the one with the golden embroidery and the silver leaf?"

"Yes," I confirmed as I took the object from his hands and gently placed it down on a wooden stool.

"So, are you gonna tell me what – or *who* – is inside the box?" David enquired in his usual caustic manner. "'Cause I'd be dying to know if I wasn't already dead."

"No one that you know, or need be concerned about," I told him firmly. "Your job was to fetch the hatbox from my residence and bring it here safely, not be made privy to its contents."

"I bet it's one of Pretorius's little homunculi, right?" my vampiric friend persisted. "I ate one of them once. Tasted sort of weird. What the hell does he use to make them things?"

"That will be all, David," I said in a firmer tone than before. "You should leave now."

But before my vampiric courier departed, he took a gander at Herbert. "Wow, what's this guy's story? Is he the love child of an orangutan and one of those jungle women? Might he be interested in a job at my carnival? 'Wild man' acts are always popular in the side shows." He turned to Herbert to address him directly. "You wouldn't mind eating live chickens in front of an audience, would you, old chap? I mean, you look like the sort who would do that."

Herbert gritted his teeth and stepped towards David. The latter's response was to widen his half-faced smirk and subtly expose his fangs. I quickly stepped in again.

"Herbert, that isn't wise," I whispered to him. "I shall see that David leaves now."

"You had best do that," the doctor of reanimation replied, "so I do not find the need to use this herculean interim body of mine to escort him out personally."

Of course, despite our low tone of voice, David's enhanced hearing had no difficulty picking it up. "Was that a challenge, hairy guy? Yippee! I *love* challenges!"

"David," I said firmly while pointing to the door. "Go. I am sure you have places to be and people to kill tonight. Perhaps by annoying them to death in lieu of draining their blood."

"Ha! I sure do," he replied. "No one is gonna see me coming in that London pea soup. But I can see through it just fine. Stay in touch, and not only when you need a favor. *Au revoir,* my forever fellow!"

With a remarkable blur of speed, David abruptly left the way he came. I was hoping that I wouldn't have a need for his services again any time soon. He does get the job done, but he raises such a ruckus in the process.

Unfortunately, as Victor and I were later to learn, David did not depart the lab empty-handed. He made a point to clandestinely purloin a pad containing some of the Baron's extensive notes featuring detailed instructions on how to graft together and animate man-made monsters. Curse me, I should have known to extract a promise from him not to take anything when I utilized his services as a courier! Victor and I would eventually have words with him about that, but, alas, not before he found a way to put that pilfered information to use. That, however, is a tale for another day, as it had no bearing on the events that this journal entry is concerned with.

"Sorry for my friend's lack of decorum," I apologized upon David's swift exit. "That is why I only invite him to certain types of parties."

"Now that that creature is thankfully gone," Victor stated, "you can explain to me why he did not come accompanied by a lady guest, as you said he would, but only brought a hatbox with him."

Herbert was staring at the container with a noticeable look of apprehension. "I believe I do know the answer to that, Baron. That is the box where... Dorian's friend Emily resided for decades. Or, rather, what was left of her."

Victor threw me a look. "Explain, Dorian."

"Why don't I simply show you instead of telling you?" I suggested.

That decided, I walked over to the box, removed its lid, and lifted up what appeared to be the strangely mutilated head of a ten-year-old girl. When I did this, she began to stir, her one good eye focusing on me as she struggled to speak through a mouth with portions of the jawbone missing or exposed.

"Dorian?" she muttered in a girlish but rough voice, as talking was by now quite difficult for her. "Is... that you? Am I... out of the box now?"

"Yes, luv, it's me," I replied in as soft and soothing a tone as I could muster. "Everything is going to be all right. I had you brought to a place where there are two men who can help you. One of whom you already met a few months ago." I turned the stool around so she could see Herbert.

"I think that is... Dr. West," she said. "But... he's gotten lots... hairier than I remember."

DORIAN GRAY VS. REANIMATOR
Body Politics
Christofer Nigro

The good doctor's eyes nearly burst from their sockets at the sight he had believed he would never see again. "But... you told me that she had... truly expired. You told me that was your reason for removing me from my practice with Dr. Hip and subjecting me to... this."

"And so I believed at the time," Dorian replied with a scathing tone. "She had gone silent for quite a while. But I kept her head, for I could not bear to dispense with it.

"But then, just a few days ago, I noticed what remained of her lips... moving. I spoke to her, and after several minutes of such verbal prodding she replied, albeit with much difficulty. The sight was too much for even the hardened housekeeper Mrs. Hartill to endure, so I had to let her go for a period of hospitalized rest.

"I should have realized that those with our enchantment do not part easily with the Earthly plane, no matter our physical state. Yet, her condition is quite grave, and I fear I will truly lose her if radical action is not taken at once. Having you in my... custody, and recalling a debt recently incurred to me by the Baron, I was struck with the realization that the pair of you were precisely what was required to help me make things right with poor Emily."

With all of that explained, Herbert's expression clearly evoked the emotions he felt when he first met this poor lady. Yet, he did his best to find a few simple words for a response in deference to her horrid condition.

"Hello again, Emily."

His voice and countenance betrayed his observation that her only remaining body part was in even worse shape than he had last seen it. She was barely coherent at this point, which was in marked contrast to the mocking spiel she had delivered to him before. Were the particles of her brain finally beginning to dissemble along with the substance in the head of the doll which her life force was tethered to?

100

That was when Victor interjected. "Is this little girl one of yours, Dr. West?"

"No," Herbert replied. "In actuality, she is one of Dorian's. She acquired a form of immortality at the young age of ten by similar means to his. In her case, however, the girl's likeness was rendered onto a doll she once owned, not on a canvas. When she later lost possession of it, her real body became subject to whatever progressively harsh treatment was meted upon the doll by its new owners through the years, particularly after it likely ended up at the bottom of a discarded pile of toys."

"Truly tragic," Victor said. "I noted the affection you showed this girl, Dorian. Which makes it obvious that you want Dr. West and I to help liberate her from this ghastly predicament by providing her with a new body that is not connected to the condition of that doll."

"You must truly have been a Great Detective in another life, Victor," I quipped. "Holmes himself would be proud."

"Do not mention that name," he said, "for I had run afoul of that one soon after one of my... mood swings got the better of me, and I... vented my rage on the ladies of the night by taking on the M.O. of the White Chapel killer."

"You mean, that Holmes fellow is real too?" Herbert asked.

"Unfortunately, yes," I answered. "I've run into the blighter myself and since then I have gone out of my way to avoid coming to his attention. And I dare say that if blokes like the three of us can be real, why *not* a man like Holmes?"

"And are you saying, Baron, that *you* were Jack the Ripper?" was Herbert's next query.

"I was *one* of those who took on the guise in the wake of whomever the original was," Victor responded, "though his story is a rather complicated one from what I could ascertain. But I may not have been to blame for that, because I had quite possibly become possessed by some fiendish disembodied entity that drove me to those acts."

"I'm certain that was it, Victor," I retorted with more than a bit of sarcasm. "After all, it's not as if your erratic 'moods,' as you call them, have ever led you to commit selfish acts of murder, extortion, and even rape when you are at your worst." I grinned. "Oh, wait…"

"Enough, Dorian!" the Baron exclaimed. "I need not be reminded of my less honorable acts when the 'fury' takes over my faculties. The lot of us in this room are complicated gentlemen, filled with many shades. Let us now confer on what the three of us may do to resolve this girl's harsh predicament and get this matter over and done with so that you can all be on your way and leave me to my work."

***

Herbert and Victor are nothing if not efficient, for within thirty minutes the three of us had formulated a plan, with each having an essential role to play to get poor Emily out of her horrifying situation. We had to move quickly, as we were quite aware that *anything* at *any moment* might happen to the remains of the doll that the unfortunate lady's life force was bound to, wherever in the world it may now be.

This was my chance to do something truly noble and selfless for once, for someone who had shown affection and kindness to me and all others she had met in the past. Some say I have no heart, but if that is the truth, then whatever I may have in its place was hurting at the sight of Emily's ordeal. I would make this right, and perhaps my conscription of Herbert and Victor to the task, two unstable men who are likewise on the bad side of karma, can likewise have a rare opportunity to channel their expertise into the salvation of an innocent instead of inflicting nightmares upon them.

DORIAN GRAY VS. REANIMATOR
Body Politics
Christofer Nigro

"Here is what we will do," Victor explained. "I am going to acquire the body of a young adult woman. You said that Miss Emily would prefer that to the body of a child?"

"Yes," I replied. "She achieved her immortality at the age of ten and became trapped at such a physical state of development over the course of several decades as a result. This caused her no small amount of frustration as the time went by. She would want an adult body, but most certainly not an old and decrepit one to precisely match her chronological age. This will give her a chance to escape from the appearance of childhood but live a full life, even if she is now fated to begin aging naturally from that point onwards."

"This is understood," Herbert said. He had now taken to wearing a lab coat over his new body, to hide its hairy grotesqueness from the sight of others – and from himself whenever he walked by a mirror. Only his original head and his normal-looking pair of hands were visible. "The Baron will procure such a body and I will use his abundant lab equipment to formulate some of my reagent. We do not want to take the chance of charging the body with galvanic energies and risk damaging it, nor with Victor's own rejuvenation chemicals, which would take some time to work and may fail if not backed up by a voltaic energy surge. Fortunately, my reagent allows us to circumvent the galvanic energy requirement."

"But you cannot graft her original head – or what is left of it – onto the new body," I pointed out. "Moreover, even if you did, we know what state of mind the body will be in once your reagent restores its physical functions. We further cannot rely on one of Victor's brain transplants, as we have no idea what shape Emily's cranial organ may be in at this point in her deterioration. So, what we need to do is to transfer not her corporeal pate to the new body or her brain into its skull, but what may best be referred to as transferring her soul out of that mutilated head and into the new body."

"I have never had, well, faith that the soul exists," Herbert admitted, "or that consciousness is a result of anything other than complex neurological processes. But the Baron says that he has had some experience with isolating an energy-based center of consciousness that departs a body upon its death and trapping it in a dense electromagnetic field. To me, this suggests that imprints of one's biological thought patterns and memories may be duplicated in the form of electrochemical impulses that power the brain. Hence, they then can potentially exist independently from their biological source material, even taking up 'refuge' in the material body of another and suppressing or forcing out the native consciousness."

"I can attest to this," I noted, "as I have recently had my consciousness transferred into the body of another, and then back again to this one. It *can* be done, so the plan is to extract Emily's consciousness – her soul, if one prefers – from the remains of her head, keep it from passing beyond our reach by trapping it in the field generated by Victor's machine, and then projecting it into a young female cadaver immediately after Herbert revitalizes its organs and tissues with an injection of his reagent."

"But where can we find a fresh female corpse of a young adult age for Emily?" Herbert queried. "London is not my usual grounds, so I wouldn't know where to acquire one."

"Worry not, gentlemen," said Victor, "for I already have that issue covered."

***

"It would seem we are in luck this evening," Victor noted as he walked into one of the branch chambers of St. Ives's extensive basement and now makeshift lab. He wheeled out a metal surgical table and pulled a cover off it to reveal a fresh young female cadaver. "Ah, the benefits of serendipity, eh my fellows?"

Both Herbert and I walked up to the corpse to inspect it up close. For one thing, the cause of death was immediately evident by the dark purple splotches on her neck along with her eyes and her swollen tongue bulging from her mouth. This lady was obviously strangled to death in a most brutal manner. And it apparently occurred a day previous, at most.

Secondly, I recognized her.

"This is Mabel, one of my favorite ladies at Madam Cossette's bordello!" I proclaimed. "I had some fine times with this one. Victor, did you…?"

"Oh, no, this wasn't my doing," the Baron hastened to answer. "You see, I'm afraid that Mabel was also Father Pence's favorite lady at Madam Cossette's place. She stormed into the church yesterday in a volatile state, barely after Pence's congregation had departed, and accused him of handing her a counterfeit 20£ banknote for their 'session' the evening before. He denied it, and this may have been the truth, as one of his congregants may have thrown the fake note into the collection plate as a lark.

"However, she was unconcerned about whether the pastor had tried to deliberately cheat her or not; she wanted to be paid the rest of what he owed her then and there. The collection plate was small that day, so he promised to compensate her the following Sunday. This offer was unsatisfactory to her, and she began raising a rumpus.

"Father Pence was desperate to silence her and, well… you see the end result lying before you now. He agreed to reimburse Cossette for her loss and to cover up the episode at his own expense. He did this by giving her remains to me. It was a double benefit in my case – more raw material to work with and yet another matter to hold our esteemed pastor to the deal he made with me."

"Dear Lord," I whispered, despite having no right whatsoever to say that.

"That would seem to be the perfect vessel for Emily's consciousness," Herbert said, "except that the larynx and trachea are likely crushed. She would be unable to breathe and may also find herself rendered mute."

"You need not worry about either eventuality," Victor assured us. "I can and will repair all damage to her throat. While I am doing that, Dr. West, you will take that time to formulate a high-efficiency version of your reagent. I am certain you will find my lab sufficiently equipped for that purpose. If not, let me know what additional components you may need, and I shall order them. They will arrive here promptly."

"Of course," Herbert replied while looking around the workshop. "I see no lack of resources for my purposes save for one ingredient... I need a few live lizards. Iguanas, monitors, or geckos will be best."

"Consider it done within the hour," Victor said. "I shall immediately telegram an order from a reliable seller of reptiles."

I refrained from asking either of them a few obvious questions. I was too concerned about Emily. Yes, you read that correctly... *concerned.*

There was always something special about her that brought out whatever there is inside of me that is most closely equivalent to decency. I do not want to see her lost to the world or be denied the second chance at life she so richly deserves. Unlike myself, her decades of unaging life were filled with far more horror and pain than fun and opportunity, and I must rectify this grievous injustice.

"While you two take care of that," I added, "I will make my own contribution, one that involves the matter of transporting her soul from where it is now to where we want it to be." I reached into my coat pocket and produced what looked like a large bronze key with tiny exotic sigils inscribed into the metal. "Behold... dear Emily's salvation."

Herbert looked quite taken aback at the sight. "Is that... one of the *silver keys?*"

"Are you colorblind, old friend?" I retorted. "No, it is not one of those, so do calm yourself. This is a recreation of a similar arcane object used by someone I recently and regretfully met who utilized it to switch bodies with me; we shan't be shanghaied to the Dreamlands with it. This version of the key will not work only for him, however. I found someone who could make this for me at considerable cost – though, as it turned out, more to herself than to me."

"I shall take your word for that, Dorian," Victor said. "In the meantime, allow me to send a courier to bring us what Dr. West needs, and let us both get on to our respective tasks."

I nodded in agreement as Victor picked up his scalpel and held it in that most unsettlingly confident and professional manner of his for a second before using it to cut into a cadaver's flesh, as if taking a moment to gauge precisely where and how to best slice for maximum efficiency. It reminded me much of how a cat will momentarily glare intensely at a spot it intends to leap onto as if precisely calculating the move first.

I walked over to poor Emily's now quiet head where it was resting in her hatbox. I gently ran a finger through a ringlet of her remaining brown hair and spoke softly to her.

"Please hold out for me just a short while longer, my dear girl," I said. "I have two... *friends* of considerable talent hard at work here to help me liberate you from this horrible condition and give you a whole new body. One that is as beautiful on the exterior as was your soul before the madness wrought by your worsening circumstance set in. A body that is young but also grown up. Just another day or so, and the vile injustice done to you by the Fates shall be set aright."

The portion of Emily's tiny lips that remained intact moved just a bit in response, but what she said was not quite audible. I looked at my two mates going about their work on her behalf for some self-reassurance.

"Please bear with us, Emily. My two friends and I will combine our efforts to make you well in just a day."

I should have known better, of course.

END PART I

PART II: THE FINAL PROBLEM

Dorian Gray's Journal, a few hours after the previous entry, mid-January 1922

"The damage to the throat is repaired," Victor announced after finishing up his stitching. I walked over to see a few sutured incisions around the bruises of poor Mabel's cadaver. "Your girl shall be able to breathe normally, albeit with a bit of pain until she has fully healed, as soon as her consciousness wakes up in that body. She will also be able to speak, but again, with some difficulty until the healing process is complete; a process that I presume will begin once Dr. West revitalizes this carcass with his reagent."

"Alright," I replied as I reached into my pocket to procure the key that was… well, the key to this entire endeavor. "Can you ready that machine of yours to 'trap' her soul in whatever type of electrical field it generates after I use this item to extract it from her head?"

"I calibrated the induction module and connected it to the galvanic generator hours ago," he informed me. "All I need do is pull the lever and give its engine a few minutes to fully charge. I will let you know when it is ready for use."

I turned to Emily's poor mutilated cranium sitting silently on the stool. *Just a few more minutes, my dearest girl. Hold onto what you have left only until then.*

Next, I switched my attention to the other doctor in my midst, who was busy at work on the other side of the lab, the bulky form he now wore barely visible to Victor and me behind the array of equipment. "How goes things on your end, Herbert?"

DORIAN GRAY VS. REANIMATOR
Body Politics
Christofer Nigro

"As well as can be expected with this awkward excuse for a body the Baron affixed my head to," he complained. "Our esteemed Dr. Frankenstein says these hands were transplanted from a sculptor. One might think he would have taken the time to find a surgeon to kill for the required parts instead. He evidently could manage such a thing to find a suitable brain in the past, but not any other portion of the anatomy, it would seem."

"Mind yourself, Dr. West!" Victor exclaimed. "That body is sufficient to do the job. I know how to select proper parts, and your acumen as a chemist should speak for itself no matter what form you now wear."

Herbert's expression took on a combative mien, so I quickly interjected with much anger. "For God's sake, gentlemen, need I remind you that this is *not* the time for that?" Then my tone softened. "Please. Play nice. For Emily."

Victor and Herbert exchanged glances. "Very well," they responded to me in tandem.

"Herbert...?" I continued.

"I managed to create enough of my reagent in its purest form to fill one syringe," he said. "That is all we require for our purposes here."

He dipped the needle into the small flask containing his iridescent green, life-restoring fluid and pulled back on the plunger to fill the glass barrel of the syringe in full. This was followed by a slight downward push on the flange to eject any excess air from the hypodermic.

"All is in readiness on my part," Herbert said.

"Good," was all I could say in response as I carefully carried the stool holding what was left of Emily just a meter in front of the metal table holding Mabel's corpse. It was soon to be my dearest's new home – courtesy of the loudly humming machine generating a powerful invisible field that would capture and hold her essence so it would not flee the mortal plane.

I struggled against being overtaken by anxiety and thus ruining the concentration required of me to focus my will through the key to extract Emily's consciousness and project it into the confines of the awaiting energy field. Rarely have I been so nervous about much of anything, but the stakes were truly high this time... and for once, I was doing something for someone other than myself.

"Can you not use that implement to simply project her consciousness directly from her head into the cadaver?" Herbert asked.

"No, as I will be too drained after getting it to Point A," I hastily answered. "I must allow myself some recovery time before moving it to Point B, which also requires different words. Now, please, be silent and let me concentrate! I mustn't forget those words!"

I cannot foul this up. Victor and Herbert both did their parts; do not let me be the link in the chain that breaks. Do not let me be the one in the assemblage that fails to hold up his end. I... must...focus...

Those thoughts flowed through my mind while I pointed the key in the direction of the head, visualizing my intention and muttering the appropriate arcane words that I had memorized to the letter. *Or did I forget some of them? Did I pronounce one or two of them improperly? No, I must stop thinking that... I will not fail Emily...*

Suddenly, the unseen field in the center of Victor's contraption began making a sizzling sound while emitting what looked to be arcs of electricity. In the middle a ball of light, roughly the size of a basketball, became visible, just hovering there.

"Dorian, you did it," Victor said. "That glowing sphere is Emily's essence. We have it. It is freed from the severely damaged remains of her original body. There it will stay

DORIAN GRAY VS. REANIMATOR
Body Politics
Christofer Nigro

until I turn off the resonator... or we direct her consciousness into a new vessel. I have managed to do that before using another setting on the machine, but not without... certain side effects."

"Just keep your contraption on for another minute," I instructed. "I need only catch a second wind, concentrate again as before, and direct Emily's essence into Mabel's intact remains. Herbert, you must inject the body with your reagent as soon as I give you the signal with my left arm. Do not risk doing so even a second sooner or later."

"I stand ready," he responded while holding up the filled hypodermic as if wielding a sword in preparation for striking down a dragon.

The key was pointed, and I focused again, mumbling the slightly different words from a long-lost language that corresponded to the characters etched onto the object's bronze metal, one set of invocations inscribed on each side. After doing this and focusing as strongly as I could, I suddenly "felt" as if an invisible harpoon had been projected from the key and attached itself to Emily's soul suspended within that field of energy. I then turned and pointed it towards Mabel's carcass.

I gave the signal with my left hand, and Herbert moved quickly to the task. He injected the reagent into the cadaver's neck.

"Approximately one minute before reanimation, Dorian," he informed me, his warning quite implicit: unless a soul took control of that body we would soon have a psychotic reanimate to contend with, as the resurrected Mabel would no longer be quite herself, to say the least.

"Victor, turn off your machine! Now!" I shouted.

He did so, and I quickly uttered the last few words in a language that was ancient when humanity was young. I heard a loud zapping sound as the energy field fizzled out and the glowing sphere representing Emily's soul flew towards Mabel's shell like a surge of electricity being drawn down an invisible wire from one point to another. The radiant orb seemed to be absorbed into the cranium of the cadaver. Afterwards, it lay silent.

Did it work? Let there be a sign...

On schedule, the reagent took effect and the young lady's body abruptly sat up with a loud gasp. Victor and Herbert moved forward with the intent to restrain the reanimated vessel if it turned out that all did not go as intended. I moved in concert with them and reached out my hand to the trembling girl.

"Emily...?" I spoke. "It is I, Dorian."

At first, the reanimated form of Mabel looked around confused, her mouth agape as if to scream. She then looked down and seemed surprised to see that she had arms and a body. When she noticed the ample breasts present on this form's chest, she excitedly squeezed them a few times, as if to confirm they were real.

"Yes, Emily," I uttered softly. "We found you a new body, as promised. One that is young, but a *grown woman* with such a body's natural... accouterments."

She then turned and looked at me. The girl was still quivering as might a person suffering from hypothermia, but her shock and fear seemed to slowly subside upon viewing my familiar countenance.

"Dorian... can it truly be you?" Her voice was a trite raspy, as Victor told us it would be, yet fully coherent. And Mabel's sultry voice never sounded more wonderful than when it began producing Emily's words.

"Yes, dearest," I replied with a smile and moistened eyes. "It is I. And everything is wonderful. Life is wonderful!"

"Oh, dear God!" she shouted with misty-eyed elation as she leapt off the table and ran into my arms. We embraced warmly as tears of joy trickled down both our faces.

"It would seem our task is successfully completed," Victor stated to the room while removing his white surgical gloves.

"Let us hope so," Herbert added quietly.

***

After spending almost a full half hour admiring her beautiful new young but adult body, including running her hands through its bright red locks and looking at the full bosom that was now finally hers, Emily walked over to Victor and gave him a quick hug. Not one for expressing affection, he barely returned it.

"Thank you so much, Baron," she said. "I shall never forget what you did for me."

"Think nothing of it," he replied. "With this, I am now free from any debt to Dorian."

"Partially," I was quick to remind him.

"And thank you also for this exquisite dress," Emily continued with her accolades. She truly was a vision in the rose-colored G&E Spitzer evening gown, particularly when she giddily twirled around in it so that its lower part billowed about like a blossoming petal. "Wherever did you come by attire like this, good sir?"

"That was once the property of Father Vasak, from the church up above," Victor noted. "My discovery of his closet full of such garments constituted another bit of leverage I acquired over the clergy of this cathedral that enabled me to secure this space for my lab."

"Of course, it did," I remarked.

"Oh, but I would be remiss to take even such a lovely gown from its rightful owner..." Emily said.

"Worry not, my dear girl," the Baron rejoined. "With a couture collection of that size, I doubt Father Vasak will even miss it. And it looks far more exquisite on you than on

114

him, trust me. Especially when you consider that he is a man of such size that he can pass for Dr. West's twin in the latter's current incarnation."

"Shut up, Baron," was Herbert's counter.

"And speaking of Dr. West!" Emily said with another spurt of youthful jubilation that matched her new outer form but belied the age of the soul within. "I need to properly thank you as well!"

She ran to Herbert and attempted to embrace him but could not quite get her arms fully around the hulking body he now possessed courtesy of Victor's surgical expertise.

"Thank you, thank you *so!*" she cheerily exclaimed.

"As the Baron said, think nothing of it," he responded while returning her embrace with evident coldness. "Because this likewise squares me with Dorian. In fact, I would say that he now owes *me.*"

"I am sure Dorian will be more than happy to offer whatever we have for your part in my liberation!" Emily jubilantly stated. "Is there anything we can do for you?"

I rolled my eyes in exasperation, but declined to protest, as I did not want to ruin the first day Emily had in decades that was not a constant nightmare. But I knew Herbert wouldn't be one to politely decline such an offer.

"As a matter of fact, my dear girl," he said, "I would be much obliged if you and Dorian would offer me room and board at your house for just a few days, while I contact a friend to come and offer me transport home. I will be bringing nothing with me but a bag of lab overcoats that the Baron has generously allowed me to take."

"Why, of course!" she said with a smile. "We can most surely accommodate Dr. West for a week or so until his friend comes to pick him up. Right, Dorian?"

I wanted to take a chance and punch Herbert directly upon his sniggering face in response, as he knew *exactly* how I would feel about such an imposition. But I did not want to

115

do a single thing to wipe that smile off Emily's lovely new visage, not after her literal inability to do so for such a long time prior to the past hour.

And I supposed that I did perhaps owe him *that much* for his help in this. Moreover, I have tolerated worse company for longer periods of time. After all, I had spent lengthy stretches in the trenches during the Great War, including the span in Flanders where I had to deal with that wanker Blackadder as a captain.

"Yes, we can accommodate Herbert for a *short* spell," I agreed, with notable emphasis on a certain word in that sentence.

"Oh, Dorian, my love!" Emily shouted with another smile. "You are truly a wonderful man!"

She ran and embraced me again, only this time she made a point to press her lips against mine and leave them there for several seconds. The act was most certainly not unpleasant, but it had a lot of clear affection behind it of a sort that I was not certain I shared.

That was to be the first sign that trouble was afoot. But I, unfortunately, shrugged off the concern as she, Herbert, and I departed Victor's clandestine lab.

***

The three of us walked back into the house situated alongside the Thames that had long belonged to Emily's family. She was excited upon seeing the place from the mobile vantage point which her new form now allowed her.

"Oh, it looks just as I remember it!" she squealed with delight, her voice now having grown less scratchy; Herbert's reagent was clearly providing a fast healing experience for Emily's new body.

"Indeed," I replied. "I made the effort to fix up the house in anticipation of your return. Mrs. Hartill is still away in…

convalescence, and I fear we must take a bit of time to figure a way to explain to her the, erm, changes with you before she can return to service here. But in the meantime, the estate is in tip-top shape."

"Dorian, dear, thank you soooo much for upkeeping it while I was… indisposed. We had such fine times here before my debilitation truly set in because of that accursed doll. I never should have allowed Basil to capture my image in that fashion."

"Nonsense, dearest," I said in response. "You are revived with a stunning young adult body to match the woman within, and all the horror is now behind you."

"Yes, it is," she agreed. Then she kissed me deeply again and ran to where she knew a large mirror was attached to the wall. "Oh, just look at this, Dorian! If only the scars on the neck heal fast. And those stitches…"

"Victor said they will heal quickly," I replied, still a bit taken aback by that second kiss she gave me in such a short time. "Now that you are extricated from your previous body, however, you will no longer heal from injuries with the same type of speed and completeness as before, for the doll shall no longer absorb them for you. As for the stitches, any doctor can remove them, which Victor said we can have done in about a week's time."

"You have a doctor at your service right here," Herbert noted as he plunked the carrying case the Baron had allowed him to take on the dining room table. "I can remove the stiches myself before I leave."

"Thank you sooooo much again, Dr. West!" Emily shouted with sizable glee as she ran from the mirror and back into my arms. "Dorian and I are so lucky to have you as a friend, good sir!"

"Again, think no more of it," he responded while opening the case. Inside of it was a set of long lab smocks to cover his now apish body, as he had noted back at the lab. But what was also there was something else he had not mentioned... a syringe filled with his green reagent chemical.

"Herbert, did you not say that you were only able to formulate but a single flask of your reagent with what you had on hand at the lab?" I queried.

"Indeed, I did," he confirmed. "I was not about to let the Baron know that I was actually able to synthesize an additional dosage beyond the one we needed. He would have insisted that I leave samples for his scrutiny. I am not inclined to share my discovery with him at this time."

Emily giggled at the revelation. "What a charming schemer our Dr. West is, eh, my love?"

I rolled my eyes. "Yes. Ever the schemer," I replied with a less ecstatic tone.

The revitalized young lady then wrapped her arms around me. She stared into my eyes with two lovely green oculars of her own that she had inherited from another woman. "Dorian, I am sure Dr. West would agree to retire to his room and give us some time with each other, right?"

"Of course," he answered with a mock smile. "Just let me know where it is located."

"Down the hall to the left of the kitchen," I quickly interjected.

That said, he was off, leaving his locked case on the dining room table. With the privacy we were now afforded, I realized that I had better do what needed to be done before any lines were crossed that bode no good outcome.

"Emily," I said, interrupting another attempted kiss from her. "You know how dear to my heart you are... how dear you have always been to me. But..."

Just then there was a knocking at the door. "People can have such inconsiderate timing!" Emily griped.

I silently disagreed with her. "I had best find out who that is. It could be important."

"Why? Are you expecting a package? Or... a visitor?"

By that point, I had reached the door and opened it, hoping it was a postal worker delivering the new broadsword I had recently ordered. The parcel containing it was indeed handed to me, but not by an employee of the post office. Rather, it was by Clarice, perhaps my favorite lady from Madam Cossette's bordello next to Mabel, one who had developed an extra-transactional interest in me and had begun visiting me here for free-of-charge trysts. Now I could not help but agree with Emily. Some people did have simply wretched timing.

"Dorian, I found this package at your door!" she said while stepping in, not thinking I would have any objection to it. "The postman must have made a late-night delivery and didn't bother to knock or ring the bell. I happened to see it lying there on the way to Cossette's place and I thought I would let you know it had arrived… and provide you with a visit from *me* as a bonus!"

I put the parcel containing the sword down on a nearby end table and turned back to Clarice. "Thank you, but I am afraid this is not the best time for a visit, dear. I am not alone here…"

That was when Clarice turned to see Emily standing in the sitting room, who gave her an utterly demonic glare in response. One could not expect the former to think she was looking at anyone other than Mabel, her fellow employee and friend, whose body had now been taken over by the consciousness of another.

"Oh, Mabel! There you are!" Clarice said while cheerfully running over to the lady who was not whom she had thought her to be. "Madam Cossette and the rest of us have been so worried about you! Where have you been for the last two days? And what happened to your neck? Why did you have to get stitches?"

Clarice stood speaking to the familiar face that did not share the recognition. Emily had by now realized what had happened, and she had been cogent enough a decade ago to learn what Madam Cossette's place was. However, she had not known until this moment that I patronized the brothel on a regular basis. It was a revelation with implications that only now became clear to her. Emily gritted her teeth, and her right fist was clenched and quivering with unwavering rage. Clarice was both startled and baffled.

"Mabel, what's wrong, dear?" she asked again. "You look as if... you might want to kill someone."

I rushed over to intervene. "Do you mean that you and Madam weren't informed, Clarice? Two days ago, Mabel was accosted by a ruffian with a knife, and her throat caught the worst of it. I took her to a hospital to get stitched up and let her stay here to recuperate. It seems the courier whom I paid £3.00 to deliver a message to Madam Cossette failed to do his job. Just wait until I lay eyes on him again!"

"Oh, you poor dear," Clarice said to Emily with a sorrowful tone. "I am so sorry that happened. Once you are well enough to return to work, you, me, and Dorian can have fun together like we always have… just the three of us. How does that sound?"

Emily's lips were now trembling with rage, and she was on the verge of exploding with the fury of an active volcano. I knew it was imperative that I get Clarice out of that powder keg and do my best to explain to Emily what the true Dorian Gray is like and find a way to make her understand and accept that reality.

Little did I know at the time – but would later learn – that Herbert was then peeking out of his room and observing the proceedings. I can only imagine the satisfied grin he had on his face, with his thoughts likely being along the lines of, *"It would seem you have a way of ruining everyone's life, Dorian. Good. Maybe this will work towards my desire for delivering to you the retribution you so richly deserve."*

DORIAN GRAY VS. REANIMATOR
Body Politics
Christofer Nigro

"Actually, Clarice, Mabel has decided to quit your... vocation as a result of this experience!" I hurriedly said while shifting my body between the two ladies. "She is unable to speak right now because of the injuries to her throat, so she wrote that information down to me yesterday."

"But... Mabel doesn't know how to read or write," Clarice said almost under her breath.

Damn it all to Hell! I wish I had known that!

"I meant, she dictated it to me with her finger signs!"

"But, I don't understand..."

"And right now, she is in too much pain to have visitors," I hastily interjected. "This is why you see that agonized expression on her face. I must give her a touch of morphine and then get her into bed. So, you should go now, and I will be in touch."

"Well... alright," were Clarice's final confused words as she strode out of the house.

That left me to speak to Emily one-to-one again. No sooner had I turned around to do so than she struck me in the side of the face, a punch that sent me down to the floor. I am not sure if Herbert's reagent had any enhancement effects on Mabel's body, but that blow was quite strong. And the action was *very* unlike the Emily I once knew.

"You... you *cad,* you!" she screamed at me out of her new set of lungs. "How dare you betray me in such a way, Dorian! *How dare you!*"

"I... did not betray you, Emily," I asserted while nursing the swollen jaw that was already repairing itself courtesy of my fabled portrait. "I was never the man you thought I was, true, but I always cared deeply about you. We had..."

"We had and have *nothing!*" she shouted before kicking me across the face, sending me sprawling onto my back. "I have always loved you, Dorian! *Always!* I waited for you all these decades while being trapped in a childish body that kept falling into more and more pieces. The only hope I ever had during that lengthy nightmare was that you were waiting for me to find a way out of that horrid little body and into one of an attractive *woman*!

"I thought your heart was true to me after you continued to care for me throughout all those years... despite your frequent extended absences for traveling the world and fighting in the war. And when you finally got me out of that wretched body and into this fabulous new one, I thought you did it not just for me, but for *us!* And now I find out that all along you had been laying with whores! *Multiple whores!* Probably wherever you set foot across the world!

"And that you even gave me the body of one of those harlots! I can scarcely imagine how many times this body has been run through by filthy men! Men whom she gave access to her most sacred part for money! *For money!* And you were among the filthy bastards who did so!"

"Emily... please try to understand," I pleaded as I got back to my feet, all the injuries she had inflicted now fully healed. "You know that attacking me like this is futile. Let us talk. I may not have been the man you thought I was all that time, but the man I really am still cares for you. Just... just not in the way..."

"Of course not! You are incapable of caring for another person as I am!" She buried her lovely face in her hands and began sobbing uncontrollably. "I cannot deal with this right now. I... I need to go to my room – my old room – and sort things out. Please... just leave me alone."

"Very well. We can talk later, and we will sort this out, I promise."

From there she ran into her bedroom and slammed the door shut. I then retreated to my own room to contemplate a resolution to this awful situation.

But leaving Emily alone like that was my next big mistake. And the one that brought this whole matter to an apocalyptic catastrophe.

***

Everything I write in this section of my memoirs was a combination of things I was later to learn and certain matters I could readily piece together based on the evidence at hand.

Upon retreating to my room, hoping that things would be better for Emily after a good night's sleep, I was to learn that she never slept at all. Instead, she quietly left the house and headed to Madam Cossette's bordello, a nearby location that everyone in her neighborhood had long known about.

She entered the premises pretending to be Mabel, the young woman once employed there who, unbeknownst to her former boss and fellow workers, had been killed and her body subsequently taken over by the mind of another woman. Despite the abject state of rage now consuming her, Emily possessed a consummate resolve built over decades of enduring an ordeal that the average person – or even immortal – could scarcely imagine. She now utilized this powerful will to conceal those volatile emotions beneath an outwardly friendly demeanor.

You see, Emily knew she could not subject me to mortal harm due to my portrait. But now that the madness which had consumed her due to her ordeal had been fully reignited, she felt a need to inflict that harm on someone else. And she had made her choice of who it would be.

"Yes, it is true that because of the attack I have chosen to give up this line of work and become a seamstress," she said to Madam Cossette at the front desk, trying to speak with a minimum of verbiage to cover for the fact that she did not know Mabel's speech patterns. "But I wanted to say goodbye to everyone in person and speak to Clarice, if I may."

"We will be sorry to see you go, my dear," I was later to learn that Cossette had told her. "You did good work for the

123

place. Might a bigger percentage of the take your customers bring in help you to reconsider?"

"I am sorry, but no. Thank you for the offer, though. May I see Clarice? Or is she… with a man?"

"Very well, dear. And you know the place will still be here should you ever change your mind after finding out how poorly a seamstress gets paid. As for Clarice, no, she finished with her last client an hour ago and is resting up in her room."

"And her room would be…?"

"You don't remember? You spent much time in there, both fraternizing with Clarice and while sharing clients."

"My apologies, but I do not feel so well. I am on rather heavy dosages of morphine because of these injuries…" She slid her fingers over the visible stitches on her throat to indicate what she meant.

"Oh, of course, dear. My sincere apologies. It is the last room down there on the right."

Emily, whom Clarice still believed to be her friend, Mabel, knocked on the door to her room and pretended to embrace her warmly when she answered.

"I am so sorry for the… fit I had earlier when I was in so much pain."

"That is quite alright, my poor dear," Clarice replied with a smile. "So, you are able to talk now?"

"Yes, I can when the morphine starts working. May I show you where the attack happened in the alley between this place and the pharmacy next door? I want to help you and the rest of the girls avoid the same."

"Oh, of course! Show me."

"We should go out the back entrance, so Madam doesn't ask us questions. There is a back entrance, right? I'm sorry, but when the drug takes full effect…"

"I understand, my baby! Yes, there is. I'll lead the way."

As soon as they stepped out into the darkened alley, Emily pointed to the brick-layered side of the pharmacy next door. "There... it happened right over there."

When Clarice turned to look in that direction the woman pretending to be a friend descended upon her. Emily grasped her neck in both hands with terrific strength and smashed her face repeatedly against the wall until her forehead and nose were caved in. She then quietly re-entered the brothel and retrieved a large blanket she had noticed in Clarice's room. The murderess wrapped the covering around the body with the pulverized face and carried it on her shoulder down the block back to her house.

No one saw anything due to the short distance of the walk and the darkness of the fog-enshrouded night. Emily counted on that, of course.

***

Emily sauntered back into her house as quietly as she could with her dead guest. Hence, she did not disturb me while I was lying in my room reflecting upon my role in what had earlier occurred between us. Curse me for a fool, but I should have anticipated that she may have suffered a resurgence of her madness rather than a mere wave of sorrow. Along with the fact that she now had a strong body to act on it!

The owner of the house dragged the covered cadaver of poor Clarice behind the couch and unwrapped it. That was when she looked up to find Herbert standing before her.

"Dr. West..."

"Be calm, Emily," he said. "I can guess what your intentions are, and you will be pleased to know that I fully approve. You have my complete agreement that Dorian deserves to get what is coming to him for all he has brought down upon me, you, and to so many others during that

125

unnaturally extended life of his. Accordingly, I have opened the case containing my reagent so that you do not have to waste time breaking the lock. Would you like me to...?"

"No," I was to later learn she responded with. "Let me, please."

"By all means."

Emily brought the syringe of reagent to Clarice's battered corpse.

"The neck is the best place," Herbert advised her. "Right here, inserted into this particular vein." He touched the portion of the dead body's throat to confirm his instructions.

"Thank you, Dr. West," Emily replied while administering the injection.

***

What followed I had no need to later learn or surmise as Emily knocked on my bedroom door to get my attention while she waited for the injection to take its ghastly effect.

I stepped out of my room to see the form of a melancholy-looking young woman standing before me, and Herbert casually leaning on the far wall of the dining room with his arms folded. His snickering face, along with Emily's own impassive expression, led me to suspect that something might be terribly wrong.

"Dorian," she said, "I think we should talk now."

"Very well, luv," I answered. "But maybe Herbert should..."

"Dr. West can stay," she decreed. "He will want to see this, I am sure."

"See what?" I queried, with my befuddlement quickly being replaced by trepidation.

"Why, you receiving your long-deserved comeuppance for being the narcissistic, filthy, and manipulative bastard that you've always been; that's what!"

She timed it perfectly, for that was when my attention was diverted by the horrific scream of the reanimated Clarice. The undead lady with the horribly mutilated face rushed out from behind the couch and directly at me.

Emily's own reanimated status was clearly discernible to the walking corpse that was once Clarice, and the newly reanimated woman ignored the scorned woman standing there while coming at me with her hands outstretched like the claws of a predatory bird. She grasped me by the throat with the furious strength of one who was truly insane and slammed me back against the wall.

"What? Clarice…?" As I struggled to break her grip, I could now clearly see what had happened. The crown of her head was crushed inward and oozing blood and brain matter, and her nasal cartilage was pulped to the point of looking like just a flattened blob of gristle. These mutilations served as obvious indicators that Emily had bludgeoned her to death. Clarice's eyes were glazed over like that of all reanimates and her mouth was filled with bubbling salivary foam as she screamed with the rage of the maddened dead that was a typical result of Herbert's nightmarish brew.

"Let us see you get out of that one, Dorian," Herbert said from across the room. "It will be quite amusing to watch you try."

"You had no business taking out your rage on Clarice!" I screamed at Emily while I struggled to keep my face from being ripped off. "She was an innocent!"

"So was I, once!" Emily retorted. "And so were many others until they crossed paths with *you*, Dorian! I am what I have become all thanks to you! My life would have been normal if not for meeting you and your circle of friends! I may not be able to kill you, but I *will* hurt you! I will never try to stop finding ways to hurt you!

"And I shall kill anyone you remotely care for to make you suffer all the more! Like I have spent decades suffering

127

and will for as long as this new body continues to live, all because of *you!*"

"You found a feisty one with this girl, Dorian!" Herbert sniggered. "Ha! Ha!"

Acting quickly, I headbutted Clarice as hard as I could, further pulverizing what was left of her septum. She screeched in anguish as blood spurted from her nostrils like twin scarlet geysers. But her grip slackened only slightly, and she then lurched forward and bit a chunk of flesh out of my cheek. I cried out in agony while kicking her in the diaphragm with enough force to knock her backwards.

I then ran over to the lighted fireplace, with the still screaming Clarice in pursuit. I grabbed a heavy log from the illuminated hearth, ignoring how the flaming wood burned my hands as I knew my portrait would quickly take care of the injuries. I smashed my reanimated attacker on the side of her cranium, worsening the head wound already delivered to the poor lady when Emily killed her. I then struck her again, this time shattering her skull and brains into fragments. The berserk thing that was once a gentle young whore named Clarice fell to the wooden floor and had returned to the status of the conventional dead.

"No! No! No! You won't win this one, Dorian!" Emily yelled furiously. "I will do this myself if I must!"

She ran towards me with the speed of an Olympic sprinter and waded into me with great force. This knocked me over and back into the blazing fireplace. She held me down with incredible strength, and I cried out once more as the flames burned the flesh on the back of my shoulders, neck, and skull.

"Emily, stop this! Please! I care about you!" I petitioned her through the pain.

"You care about no one but yourself, Dorian!" she yelled back. "Now suffer at the hands of what I became for loving one such as you!"

DORIAN GRAY VS. REANIMATOR
Body Politics
Christofer Nigro

"Okay, enough of this!" I hollered as I grabbed the reddish hair that once belonged to a lady named Mabel. I used this grip to pull Emily's face over my head and into the flames behind me.

The lady squealed in agony like a branded pig as the fire burned her entire face to a blackened crisp. Her hair also caught fire much as mine did, but she had much more of that on her head to burn than I had on my own. I then positioned both my feet against her stomach and double-kicked her off me. The girl jumped to her feet screaming like a banshee with her entire head now alight like a huge tapir candle.

Emily hurtled towards the front window and jumped through the glass. She was beyond caring that the shards cut her new body to shreds, so desperate was she to find a way to douse the flames and curtail the pain now consuming her body. And the only way her tortured mind could conceive of doing so was leaping into the Thames located just several yards in front of her home.

Her screams echoed through the mist-shrouded night for a few seconds before she plunged into the darkened waters of the river. There was no sign that she had ever resurfaced. I swear there is something about that river that seems to act as a siren call for the wretched.

I pushed myself back to my feet as the horrid burns I had endured began rapidly healing, being absorbed by the arcane magick infused into my hidden portrait. That was when I was grasped in a powerful grip and smashed up against the wall with enough force to imbed my bodily shape into the plaster.

"Sorry, Dorian," I heard Herbert's voice say through the haze now enveloping me. "But now it is *my* turn."

With his head still grafted to Herr Schneider's powerful simian body, my scientist friend was more than my physical match and he proved this by delivering a hammering sock to my face that shattered my jawbone. This was followed by a blow to my sternum that fractured three ribs and punctured one of my lungs.

"I know how that cursed painting repairs all damage done to you, Dorian. So, how about we push it to its limits by inflicting more upon you than you've ever had to deal with before. More than you incurred even during the time I knew you during the Great War! You deserve no less than the worst, my good friend!"

And so, the punches continued for a relentless five minutes longer, my healing process barely able to keep up with the barrage of terrible wounds visited upon me. However, Herbert could see the terrible damage he brutally effectuated with Schneider's form beginning to self-repair almost immediately after each subsequent blow. So, he decided to take another tactic.

"You know, Dorian, I have always wondered something: Can you recover from drowning? How about you follow poor Emily into the Thames and let us see how well your ensorcelled portrait pulls you out of that sort of predicament!"

Herbert lifted me over his head as if I weighed but an ounce and hauled me towards the artificial egress of the broken window, intent on carrying me across the street and hurling me into the river. The question he asked was a good one and not any I cared to learn the answer to the hard way. Luckily, he had made the error of underestimating the speed of my recovery.

The severe damage he had inflicted upon me had healed just enough that I was once again cognizant within a few seconds. As he carried me through the dining room, I saw us headed past the end table where my packaged new broadsword was lying. Herbert had no idea what the parcel contained, of course.

As we passed the table I reached down and grabbed the packet. I quickly tore off the paper and promptly had the shining blade in my hand. I stuck the pointed steel tip into my erstwhile friend's left calf, causing him to shout in pain and drop me to the floor.

With my injuries now further healed I jumped to my feet, the weapon in hand. But Herbert's current body was a *living* weapon, and he angrily swung his massive right arm at me. I managed to duck the blow and swing my blade around in a move I learned from one of the best swordsmen in the world. The razor-sharp cutter neatly sliced Herbert's head off Herr Schneider's ape-like body.

He released a cry of frustration coupled with agony as his cranium bounced across the rug and his now decapitated body fell to the floor in a big unmoving heap.

"Curse you… Dorian," the once again bodiless Herbert West admonished me.

"As you can see, Herbert, the wounds you gave me are now over 90% healed," I boasted. "The hunk of flesh bitten off my face by Clarice early in this imbroglio has long since been restored. This is a benefit you will not yourself enjoy."

I put my blood-covered sword down on the end table and walked towards Herbert's disembodied head "You should have stayed out of my conflict with Emily. Things would have gone easier for you if you had."

"It would have gone easier for you also, and that is why I did not. You have gone too far too many times, Dorian. Look what became of Emily for loving you. I know what happened so long ago. She asked Basil to craft her image with that enchanted paint of his so that she could live forever with you. She knew what you had become thanks to the man's magickal art. Even as such a young girl she was no fool. In fact, her youth made her more open to believing such things and recognizing real magick when she saw it.

"Just look what happened to her because of that. And look what happened to that poor, pathetic whore – Clarice, did you call her? – for fancying you!"

"I… know I am far from a paragon of godliness, Herbert. I have more regrets now than ever before, let me tell you. But you are not one to point fingers… if you still had fingers to point with, that is.

"Right now, I think I shall vent my own pain by using your head as a football. Then once I finally tire of that – perhaps several hours from now – I think I will toss it into the hearth. After all, it is unfair that Emily and I had a taste of those flames, but not you. I shall rectify that."

"I have something to tell you before you do these things, Dorian."

"Oh?"

"When the nerves of a head are joined to those of a body with the expertise of someone like Baron Frankenstein, a body that is backed up by a voltaic charge, the connectivity can be a particularly powerful one."

"My thanks for that interesting information, Herbert. A pity your mouth will soon no longer be in any condition to regale me with more such anecdotes."

"Heh. Heh. I didn't tell you that for no reason, you fool."

That was when I felt a familiar, powerful grip grasping my throat from behind and effortlessly lifting me into the air. Schneider's now headless body, its nervous system still active and under Herbert's control, hurled me clear through the door leading into the den. The thick wood of the barrier in front of it was no impediment for a man of average weight thrown with such force, and several of my ribs were re-broken along with my back upon the impact.

I was only later to learn what had occurred next. Herbert directed Schneider's body to lift him up and carry his head out into the fog-enshrouded night. He would have realized that he had to find cover quickly, as he might be conspicuous even in darkness surrounded by the misty soup.

After several minutes, I stumbled out of the den, my spinal cord now mostly repaired. My ribs had also moved

132

back into place of their own accord, and the lacerations in my lung tissue were fully sealed. I coughed away some of the residual pain and looked around.

"Herbert, you most certainly have one coming to you when next we meet," I said aloud to no one in particular.

I then stepped over Clarice's pulverized corpse to look at the shattered window and out onto the moonlit surface of the Thames. I began to weep.

Emily, I am so, so sorry...

***

Another thing I was later to learn was as follows. Roughly twenty minutes after leaving my home, Herbert had made his way several blocks distant while in the grip of the strong, ape-like body which he still controlled. Directing its movements while in a decapitated condition, especially in the dark with all the fog that was about, could not have been easy. But he was determined, and so he managed it.

His cover was soon to be more secure when he happened to spot a lone chap walking up the deserted street before him. The man's slightly wobbling pace and his offkey rendition of "Oh! What a Pal Was Mary" made it clear that he had been imbibing. He was said to be wearing a long, wide trench coat, and that was exactly what the doctor had ordered.

The chap's mouth opened with shock when he saw the hulking, blood-stained, headless figure that stepped out of the billowy nighttime mist before him.... one that carried a disembodied, talking head.

"Ummmm... Jesus, Mary... and... and..."

"Forgive me for this, my good man," Herbert stated to the stammering bloke, "but I have need of your coat."

The brutish body under his control slugged the man in the face, breaking his jaw and knocking him unconscious. Herbert then had Herr Schneider's form remove the man's weather-resistant garment and wrap it around itself, concealing both its simian appearance and the fact that it was carrying a severed, speaking head. That accomplished, Herbert directed the body to leave the area, and it disappeared into the foggy darkness.

Of course, when the nearly frozen man was discovered the next morning and taken to the hospital, and once he was able to speak again, the report he gave was written off by the bobbies as being a simple case of a drunk being accosted and robbed by a thief carrying a blackjack. The description given was taken to be the result of a mind scrambled by a combination of poor visibility conditions, severe inebriation, and the aftereffects of a serious blow to the head.

EPILOGUE

The following morning

Winslow Perkins desperately tapped out a message on his teletype machine under the orders of the demon that had broken into his small hardware shop the other night. The humble proprietor was aghast at how the infernal beast had a head like a man that was not attached to its body. And what a body it had! Its form resembled that of a gorilla more than a human, and it seemed to be rapidly bleeding out from a stab wound to its leg. Did Michael the Archangel do that with his heavenly sword right after the escape of his Monster from Hell?

"Are… are you sure you will leave me alone forever if I type and send this message for you?" a terror-stricken Winslow asked the head sitting on his counter.

"But of course," Herbert West replied. "If you do that, and then bury the body that carried me in here under the dirt floor of your garage as instructed and promise to never disturb its resting place."

"Yes! I promise! Just please… please don't hurt me and my family. We're God-fearing people, and…"

"That is good and dandy, Winslow, but keep to your task! This is important!"

"I'm sorry! I'm sorry! What did you want me to type on the telegram again?"

"Listen carefully, as I do not care to keep repeating this."

PICKMAN, RICHARD – (STOP) –

I AM STILL IN THAT CONDITION AND

CURRENTLY HIDING OUT AT A HARDWARE STORE

ON 56 FILLMORE AVENUE IN LONDON – (STOP) –

YOU MUST RETRIEVE ME WITH DUE HASTE –

(STOP) – BE QUIET AND DO NOT UTTER MY NAME

WHILE HERE – (STOP) – AVOID DORIAN AT ANY

COST

WEST

DORIAN GRAY VS. REANIMATOR
Body Politics
Christofer Nigro

END

BONUS EPILOGUE STORY:

THE PRETENTIOUS PRETORIUS

Christofer Nigro with Kevin Heim & input from Pete Rawlik

And with much inspiration from, and mad respect for, the work of Tom Sutton and Gary Friedrich

London, England 1904

Dr. Septimus Pretorius could scarcely believe whom he was now sitting with and speaking to inside his den, which was sequestered within the infamous Whitechapel district of Britain's prize city. He and the young-looking but most certainly not actually young lady were sipping hibiscus tea across from each other at a metal laboratory table doubling as a kitchen accessory. The darkness of the room was dispelled only by the light of a burning kerosene lamp. The woman's exotic beauty was marred only by a series of circular scars surrounding her neck and certain of her bodily extremities, these being an indication of the truly strange nature of her genesis. Her long, luxurious hair was thick and wavy, and the color of chestnut brown with white streaks.

"So… you believe I was once none other than Elizabeth Frankenstein herself?" the tall woman in the elegant

Edwardian high-shouldered chiffon dress enquired of her host as she sipped her tea. "The one whom his Monster murdered in a vindictive and jealous rage shortly after they were wed?"

"I do," Pretorius replied. "My research bears this out, as does my careful examination of your... erm, unique physiology. It is an oft-whispered rumor among scholars of the Frankenstein lineage that Victor Frankenstein the first created not one but two female beings as an intended mate for his Monster, albeit at different times. The first is well-attested, having been recorded in Shelley's novel; in this instance, he is said to have destroyed the female before bringing her to life, that being the incident which prompted his Monster to murder his creator's new wife, Elizabeth.

"However, as per the rumors, shortly after this and shortly before Victor's ill-fated pursuit of his Monster into the Arctic, the creature had coerced his progenitor into attempting to make him another mate. This time, however, Frankenstein had utilized part of his murdered wife's cadaver for his creation's intended. This choice was made at the insistence of the Monster, as he was quite taken with his father's fetching bride and regretted killing her in a fit of vengeful pique.

"This second instance went unrecorded by Shelley, who comprised her work from the journal entries of Robert Walton, the sailor whom Victor the first told his story to just before dying. Evidently, it was too difficult for him to discuss, even while dictating what he knew would be his final words. But rumors of this second act of creation were whispered throughout underground channels and finagled its way into certain official sources which often conflated Victor's two endeavors into creating a female flesh golem into a single action with two conflicting results."

Lily ceased sipping her beverage upon hearing that. "Really, now?"

138

"Oh, yes. But with his second go at it, it was said, Victor the first did indeed bring the female to life… though within moments of her animation, he once again succumbed to a breakdown of guilt and terror, and he stabbed her to death. The saddened Monster soon found the slaughtered form of his intended bride in his father's makeshift lab and buried her. That event, of course, was the catalyst for the final confrontations between the two that led to Frankenstein's ill-fated pursuit of his creation into the frozen North.

"Did you not tell me that one of your earliest memories was using your great strength to dig yourself out of what appeared to be a grave?"

"Yes. I do not recall seeing Frankenstein's face after I first awakened."

"That provides further credence to my resolution regarding your origins. Frankenstein's mind was so erratic upon your awakening that he did not stop to consider that you could heal even such horrendous injuries over time, much as his first Monster could. And that is precisely what you did while convalescing in a death-like state within your earthen resting place."

"But was Elizabeth truly a woman of such a height as I possess?"

"I believe not, Lily. My examination suggests that only his dear wife's head was used to create… you. It was affixed to the body comprised of several dead women likely stolen from local graves, medical schools, the gallows… or, perhaps even a few fresh kills, courtesy of the Monster.

"I hope it does not upset your delicate sensibilities to know that most of you was imported from the British Isles. But as is typical of such creations, you have no conscious memories of the woman – or women, to be most accurate – that you once were. Most interesting were the set of functional ovaries that Frankenstein appears to have found for your body."

The composite woman who now took the name Lilith 'Lily" L'Avenza turned the left side of her dark, pouty lips upwards in a quizzical fashion. "Do you mean... I can become pregnant and give birth?"

"I believe so, yes. But based on what I could discern, you will likely only be capable of bearing sons."

The expression on Lily's face now took on an intrigued countenance. "That information is most interesting to know, Dr. Pretorius. I thank you for all you have helped me learn during our short time working together."

The scientist took a sip of tea before smiling in response. "It has been my pleasure, dear lady. And most fruitful for my studies. I hope all that I have taught you will one day... bear fruit for you as well. Hopefully, in more ways than one. Heh. Heh."

***

Inglostadt, Germany 1919

Dr. Septimus Pretorius looked down at a writhing set of disembodied limbs, all divested from a bandaged body that was brutally hacked to pieces by a mob of terrified villagers. Near these parts was the head belonging to the dead yet animated body... one which the depraved but surpassingly brilliant scientist recognized as a former pupil of his. He could hardly forget those glory days many years earlier when he was an instructor at the University of Geneva and his two prize students were the Frankenstein cousins, Henry and Aloysius.

The former "got away" from the good teacher for a long time following his excommunication from respectable academia. Aloysius, however, soon looked his former instructor up and they spent some time working together after his student was awarded his scholarly degrees in surgical medicine and physics. What they created together was incredible, despite the short time it lived; and the utter failure of Pretorius to replicate his student's success without the helping hand of a Frankenstein at his side was something that had long grated him.

The severed head of Aloysius Frankenstein, which looked to have been covered with mini-lacerations and small burns, had its eyes closed despite the mouth moving as if desperately trying to utter a string of words.

Pretorius smiled before he spoke. "Do my eyes deceive me, or is that you down there amidst that moving pile of limbs, Aloysius? Or, do you prefer to be called Victor or Henry, the twin middle names you inherited from two esteemed members of your most remarkable – if most difficult to deal with – lineage?"

The mouth continued quivering as the eyes popped open. The glassy orbs appeared undamaged as they moved to glare up at the source of the chillingly familiar voice, one from an earlier part of his life that Aloysius had hoped to never again revisit.

"Do you not recognize an old friend through the beard and mustache I have grown?" the doctor queried with a wide beam. "Or is it, perhaps, the top hat and false spectacles I am wearing that presents you with some confusion? My apologies, but one bearing my reputation must be as surreptitious as possible while walking through these parts of the continent."

"Pre—Pretorius?" the head of Aloysius Frankenstein muttered with some difficulty. Was he having a pre-mortem hallucination after being hacked to pieces? He prayed this was so.

"It is good to see that your larynx still functions, my old student," Pretorius replied. "Am I correct in surmising that a second creation of yours put you in this state, then left you at the not-so-tender mercies of some alarmist villagers?"

Frankenstein's barely cognizant head struggled to respond. "I... brought life to a being... from parts of those who were... dead. Like Henry before me... and Victor so long before him..." He opened his mouth as if attempting to cough, only to find himself unable to do so due to his lacking a throat. "But... the being went... mad. Rejected me... started killing everyone I...held dear. Just like... with the first Victor's Monster. History... repeated itself... it is... the family curse."

"Your family curse?"

"Yes... it so often happens... to those who carry the blood... of this clan. As if so many of us are... forced to be pawns in... some nightmarish play that is often rewritten with... different actors... but only minor details changed. I pursued him... to Siberia. I... died. Then he... brought me back to... remains of castle. I should never... have put brain of... dead scientist in him. The wretch... remembered how galvanic... machinery worked and the proper chemicals... to inject me with. Egor helped him... attach my head to body...brought me this... freakish semblance of life... to force me to experience the horror of being... like him.

"I stumbled into village... into tavern, confused and... desperate for help. They were horrified... I was like him! Dear God in Heaven... I was now like him! The people attacked me, burned me... then cut me to pieces!

"But... I did not die. Lord help me... I cannot die! Not even in... this state. Pretorius... h—help me. Pleaaassee..."

Then the eyes and mouth went still save for the facial tics making it clear the head still lived. That it would *always* live.

Pretorius beamed with a expression of depraved glee. "So, Frankenstein, once my pupil and later my collaborator, lived to create a second golem of flesh! Fear not, thing of darkness. I, Septimus Pretorius, will make you whole once again! You will have another body! You will live to serve Pretorius!"

142

DORIAN GRAY VS. REANIMATOR
The Pretentious Pretorius
Christofer Nigro – Kevin Heim – Pete Rawlik

The scientist began cackling in raucous joy as he retrieved Frankenstein's head, along with a few choice remnants from the still animate body pieces around him.

My former student will help me duplicate his experiments with full success… even if he may need to be persuaded just a bit.

***

Almost one month later

The small, rarely used little basilica lay in smoldering ruins after being struck by torrents of galvanized electricity. This structure was located within the *Bois de Boulogne* recreational park in Paris, above a large section of the catacombs hidden deep beneath the city's famed Opera House. Prior to its destruction, it had served as the staging area for a bold experiment conducted via an alliance of Dr. Septimus Pretorius… and none other than the deadliest of all European assassins called Erik, also known as the Phantom of the Opera.

A small explosion burst through the stone wreckage and created an open chasm amidst the ruins. Out of it crawled the soot-covered but mostly uninjured duo responsible for this debacle.

"*Au diable tout ça en enfer!* It is all ruined!" Erik exclaimed in his melodic voice and distinctive French accent as he adjusted his mask to cover the skeletal deformity beneath what passed for his face. "Do you know how long it took me to put together such an organ with tuning forks that could pierce the veil of time?

"I had to procure snippets of exceedingly rare machinery left over from future eras courtesy of Doctor Omega's haphazard travels! Then I had to solicit the technical expertise of that madman Tornada to interface the device with my own musical machinery!"

Pretorius heard his own voice rising in response to the Opera Ghost's anger, as well as his frustration at how quickly his plan fell apart, once the unaccounted-for variable of a psychic girl with telekinesis was added to the mix. Remembering himself, he lowered his volume before continuing, but not his intensity.

"I contributed as much as you did to this plan, and I lost just as much as well."

"Have you so easily forgotten my own contributions? It was only through my knowledge of Crawford Tillinghast's tuning fork-based resonators that your mastery of harmonics even proved relevant!"

"I forget nothing, *docteur!* Your valued contributions pale next to the resources I provided, and lost, in this venture! Do not forget that specific vibrations are required to pierce the dimensional barriers of Tillinghast's original resonator... and how music can provide the needed harmonics."

"I am well aware of that, good sir. Not to mention being privy to the work of Erich Zann, who utilized music to accomplish much the same thing. That is why I sought you out for your mastery of the melodic arts. I understood that connecting the Tillinghast tuning forks to your sophisticated organ could provide the necessary vibratory force to pierce the membranes of time and space. Hence, both of us could achieve our goals with such a device."

"So true. But that is not to mention the additional financial expenditures I was required to pay Tornada, not only for his scientific assistance but also to procure the services of those spider-like man-midgets that his perverse experiments had fashioned. Now they are all dead too! And they were good and loyal minions!"

DORIAN GRAY VS. REANIMATOR
The Pretentious Pretorius
Christofer Nigro – Kevin Heim – Pete Rawlik

"But they made very bad coffee, Erik," Pretorius retorted. "Even with multiple arms enabling them to make several mugs at once. And it is quite uncalled for to disparage 'perverse experiments' that create bizarre forms of life, as I am apt to take that personally." The scientist smiled to further emphasize his attempt to get his partner-in-horror out of his angry funk.

"You think this is amusing, Pretorius?" The Phantom rejoined as he moved his masked visage directly up to the slightly shorter scientist's face. "You too lost everything, including the Monster and the head of Frankenstein!"[1]

Pretorius winced only a tad bit from the angry face-to-face intimidation. Erik was not one to be trifled with, but the dark physician had confronted even more dangerous entities in his day. "Yes, I am well aware of that, *mon ami,*" he replied with a less flippant tone. "But experiments fail all the time. Not all of them shall be like that, however.

"Look, for instance, at my successful creation of those homunculi, and the strides I have already begun making with the infant science of cloning. And you with that lovely trio you call the 'Angels of Music.' There will be other Frankensteins for me… and other opportunities for you to both acquire loyal minions and to pierce the time barrier in search of those unique artifacts you crave."

Since Erik knew what typically occurred when he let his notorious temper run rampant, he used his iron will to take his partner's advice and gain control over himself. *"Ah, très bien,"* he said. "Perhaps you are correct. I must salvage what I can from this wreck and begin anew."

"As must I," was Pretorius's reply.

---

[1] The whole story can be read in the "Frankenstein II" series that ran in Skywald's comic magazine *Psycho* #3-6, written by Tom Sutton (a.k.a., Sean Todd).

DORIAN GRAY VS. REANIMATOR
The Pretentious Pretorius
Christofer Nigro – Kevin Heim – Pete Rawlik

"There is… something I should perhaps tell you, *mon estimé collègue.*"

"Oh?"

"Oui. It concerns something I had witnessed when I briefly utilized a ruined but still somewhat functional 'chrono-scope' left by Omega that permitted one to view potential future events. These scenes much resembled the moving picture shows you can see in one of the theaters. You have been to them, correct?"

"No, I have not."

"Have you at least seen the moving pictures on a nickelodeon?"

"That I have."

"Very good. As I was watching the window on the chrono-scope, a moving scene involving you from a time evidently more than sixty years hence came into focus. In it I witnessed either you, or one of your family that greatly resembled you, suffering… well, quite a bizarre fate from the use of the Tillinghast technology. This had occurred – or, rather, *will* occur – alongside what appeared to be a young descendant of Tillinghast himself. So, have a care, *mon ami."*

"Really, now? How intriguing. Please do tell me as much as you were able to determine from that apparent future scenario that you viewed."

The two of them began walking into the foliage of the large park towards another clandestine entrance to the underground chambers located deep beneath the Paris Opera House that Erik and few others were privy to. As a result, they did not notice the twin forms of Dorian Gray and Baron Victor Frankenstein peeking from behind a large tree located nearly twenty meters distant. Together they had secretly scavenged the wreckage and retrieved the head of Aloysius Victor Henry Frankenstein.

DORIAN GRAY VS. REANIMATOR
The Pretentious Pretorius
Christofer Nigro – Kevin Heim – Pete Rawlik

"See?" Dorian said with a smirk. "Did I not tell you that my contacts were correct when they mentioned that a relation of yours – or part of him, leastways – was in the custody of Pretorius and that Opera Ghost killer?"

"Yes, yes, Dorian, you were," the Baron said as he looked over the unconscious head of Aloysius in his hands. The still-living cranium had been rendered insensate after first being flung around the underground lab by a display of psychic force before being violently ejected to the surface from the explosion. "His skull is fractured, and his jaw dislocated, but if the head is as resilient as I suspect, Aloysius should be good as new soon. I shall likewise suture up the many cuts all over his face and remove the spots of burned tissue, as well as that piece of glass from his left eye."

"I told you, very little harm done, and quite a bounty acquired, eh, mate?"

"Yes. I am most certainly in your debt for this very important find."

"Indeed, you are. Again."

Frankenstein sighed. "Of course, I do not expect you to allow me to forget this."

"You can rest assured I shall not until after I collect on the debt. This particular one, that is."

"I swear, Dorian, the day will come when you will find yourself in *my* debt. Everyone I know eventually does." The forever-young man smiled impishly while the Baron sighed again. "I would have liked to have discussed matters with Pretorius, without revealing that I had absconded with Aloysius's head. However, I believe it would have been imprudent for even the two of us together to confront him with the Opera Ghost present, especially when the killer was in a mood."

"I am acquainted with Erik, so I can assure you that your choice was a wise one, Victor. But let us take our leave, as I would like to visit one of the Parisian brothels before making my way back to merry old England."

***

Dunham, a small hamlet outside Montreal, Late Summer/Early Fall 1922

Herbert West was pleased to be "back together" again and to be free of any and all obligation to *Der Zirkus L'Avanza* even if his time spent assisting Lily L'Avanza was most interesting… if a bit on the messy side. As he planned on where next to go and set up his practice of the damned, he was content to simply take a day or two of respite. Accordingly, he sat enjoying an early morning breakfast of pancakes and crepes whilst sipping some fine Chardonnay wine at a quaint little Francophone restaurant called *Serviteurs de Sirop*.

Little could he predict that his quiet repast would be rudely broken when a most extraordinary individual entered the establishment and walked up to his small table sequestered in the back of the premises.

"Dr. Herbert West, I presume?" the unexpected visitor asked in a low voice.

The doctor of reanimation looked up to see a tall figure wrapped in a trench coat with a top hat and large specs adorning his face. This man bore a wide smile, but one that did not exude anything resembling cordiality; instead, it was more akin to a grin that a killer would have just before eliminating his target. Of course, West was both beguiled and alarmed that a stranger had identified him, let alone located his presence.

"Who is asking?" West queried while taking another sip of wine, determined to keep up a bold front so as not to give this interloper any psychological advantage. "If you do not mind, I am having breakfast."

"Then I shall join you," the beaming man said as he invited himself to sit down at the other side of the small table. "And to answer your question... I am Doctor Septimus Pretorius. Perhaps you have heard of me?"

Pretorius's smile widened when West's eyes bulged from their sockets, and he spilled a trickle of wine on his coat. "Ah, so you *have* heard of me then."

West did his best to look calm as he casually wiped the droplets of red liquid from his clothing and chin. *Could this truly be* him? *It must be, as few could have located and identified me so easily, let alone would have approached me so brazenly if they did know who I was. I should take advantage of this unexpected opportunity.*

"So... we meet at last," West said stoically as he put down his wine glass and offered his hand to the fellow doctor of the unorthodox.

Pretorius kept up his smile and betrayed only the slightest sign of caution as he accepted the offer of a handshake. "Heh. Indeed, indeed! So, how is the food here? I am told the French Canadians can prepare quite the feast."

"It is adequate, Doctor. Now, can you tell me how you found me? And why you have chosen to make my acquaintance?"

"But of course. Where are my manners? To answer your second question first, I received word that you had recently played a remarkable role in a most amazing birth. One which involved a mutual acquaintance, that being a lady named Lily L'Avanza."

"That is correct," West replied as he shoved another hunk of pancake in his mouth. "I also... worked for her for a time. She was responsible for having me... reassembled, as I had spent a spell in a dismembered state."

DORIAN GRAY VS. REANIMATOR
The Pretentious Pretorius
Christofer Nigro – Kevin Heim – Pete Rawlik

"Oh, I am aware of the unfortunate circumstance that you had endured for so many months! I am quite understanding, as I have long had dealings with individuals in disembodied states. Heh. Heh."

West momentarily halted the mastication of his vittles and glared at his most honored interlocuter upon receiving this news. "How were you aware of that predicament of mine?"

"I will tell you that when I answer your first question, how I located you here. But before I do that, may I ask you to tell me the particulars of Lily's birth? She had been given quite a pair of ovaries by Victor Frankenstein."

The Reanimator seemed to think the request over for a few seconds as he finished chewing and swallowing. "Very well. I must start by saying that your assessment of female anatomy is deeply flawed, as Lily informed me that you told her she would only give birth to sons. Her progeny, however, was female."

"Really? Oh, well. Now, can you please tell me the rest while sparing no detail?"

Herbert West did as requested, keeping but a few key details to himself, as he preferred no one with medical expertise other than himself to possess such knowledge. "That is all, Doctor. Now, as to my first question?"

"I thank you, and of course. Another mutual acquaintance of mine had reason to keep tabs on you following your departure from London while you were still in multiple pieces, as he had… business with you. When his information channel, along with my own, discovered news of your time with *Der Zirkus L'Avanza*, I talked him into allowing us to have this conversation upon finally locating you. As well as…"

"Who is that second acquaintance?" West interrupted with a very defensive tone.

DORIAN GRAY VS. REANIMATOR
The Pretentious Pretorius
Christofer Nigro – Kevin Heim – Pete Rawlik

"Why, that man right there," the grinning Pretorius said while pointing in the appropriate direction.

West turned to see the dandily dressed Dorian Gray standing just inside the entrance to the restaurant. "Hello, Herbert. Long time, no see, as you Americans say. Though certainly not long enough for either of us."

"Dorian..." the doctor of reanimation grumbled while grabbing a cutting knife in his hand. "Come closer and allow me to greet you properly."

"Now, now, Herbert," the young-looking gentleman said while holding out one of his hands in a gesture of appeasement. "I am well aware what each of us feels that we owe the other as a result of our last encounter. But... after telling Dr. Pretorius all about you, he has convinced me that we should not settle things in this manner, for you may be more useful to both of us intact... at least for the nonce."

"Yes, yes, Dr. West," Pretorius concurred while giving his newest consociate a few light conciliatory pats on his free hand. "So, no need to react with such vitriol."

West refused to relinquish the knife. "If you know Dorian as well as I do..."

"I most certainly do, Doctor," Pretorius agreed, "but still, for the future benefit of all three of us, I must insist that you calm down."

Pretorius blew a palmful of dust into Herbert West's face, causing him to pass out in his chair, his closed fist still grasping the sharp cutlery.

"With the proper dosage, this concoction of Farou Island soma powder could fell a gargantuan, or even a titan, but I suspect exposure to his own reagent has bolstered the doctor's constitution to far more than that of any beast. Come, we should be away before he wakes up in a sour mood again."

"Yes, yes, I have every intention of keeping my word, Tim," Dorian responded, "as much as it pains me to do so.

Now, let us be off, as we have a council meeting to attend far from here."

"Indeed. Perhaps one day Dr. West will find himself accepted into the D Club, as you and I have been. He is most certainly working towards that goal, and he has already defied death numerous times."[2]

"Yes, perhaps."

With that, the two men departed the pancake eatery. Upon walking outside, Dorian grabbed Pretorius by the tunic of his jacket to get his attention in an aggressive manner. "Pray tell, what exactly do you require Herbert's expertise on that you insisted he remain alive for?"

"It is not something I can go into much detail about at this time," Pretorius replied as he prepared to hail a cab. "Let me just say that I believe our dear Dr. West's work will prove to be quite a boon to the burgeoning science of cloning, something Dr. Tornada has already been experimenting with over in France… and which I have recently turned my own attention to.

"I believe such a form of biological replication will prove a better way to produce heirs to my legacy than having actual children. The latter method would force me to mix my genes with that of another, thus potentially diluting the quality of the progeny. I also believe that cloning will be a select means to produce some heirs for our esteemed master of reanimation himself somewhere down the line if all proves successful."

"Can you perhaps elaborate a bit on that, Edward?"

"I prefer you call me 'Septimus' or even continue calling me 'Timmy,' as you are wont to do, if 'Dr. Pretorius' is too

---

[2] See Kevin Heim's eponymous short story "The D Club" in the anthology *Dorian Gray: Darker Shades* from Wild Hunt Press for the full skinny on that most exclusive organization. Pretorius will be there… and he will be far from alone.

formal in your eyes. I never much liked that forename of mine. But now is not the time for such a lengthy discussion, as I have attracted the attention of a cab driver, and we should be well away from this location before our mutual friend awakens."

Minutes later, Herbert West found himself jostled back to consciousness by the incessant shaking of a concerned waitress. *"Monsieur?* Monsieur! Are you unwell?"

West jumped up with a start and instinctively lashed out with the knife, slicing open the pale skin of the server's forearm. She jumped back and screamed as blood seeped out of the wound.

"Oh! I am so sorry!" the physician cried as he realized his error. "I thought you were someone else. Listen, I am a doctor, and I will tend to that wound free of charge."

"No! No! Get away from me!" the horrified young waitress screamed back. "Just get out of here!"

"Alright, alright, I will do that," West said as he hastily got up to depart while dropping five Canadian one-dollar bills onto the table. "Keep the change for the trouble. And I will, um, take this knife with me, if you do not mind."

"Just get out!"

Herbert West was quickly out the door holding the bloody knife in his hand for assurance. He looked around and saw no sign of either Dorian Gray or Dr. Pretorius in the vicinity, and he was confident that both were long gone. His immediate goal was to depart the area with due haste, before the other restaurant employees rushed out after him, let alone had time to summon the authorities.

The doctor managed to hail a Montreal cab upon making his way around the block, which he paid good money to quickly take him back into the city and across the border into Vermont. The physician of the damned was determined to return to the United States to find a place to resume his practice and the nefarious research that he did on the side.

He would have to wait a long time before finding out the nature of Septimus Pretorius's plans for him.

END

If you enjoyed this tale of terror, please let the world know via a positive review on Amazon, Goodreads, your personal blog, podcast, or channel on YouTube or Rumble *et al,* or anywhere else reviews of this sort are permitted! The more such feedback and support we get, the more of these gems Wild Hunt Press can bring you, and satisfying your morbid nightmares is both our purpose and pleasure!

Also please visit Wild Hunt Press on our Facebook group & page and our Instagram, where you can likewise leave your feedback! Coming soon will be our official website and newsletter! And feel free to write us at wildhuntpress@gmail.com .

ABOUT THE AUTHORS

Pete Rawlik is a writer living in Florida where he collects Lovecraftian fiction and works on environmental issues surrounding the Everglades and related ecosystems. His research for a pseudo-history of the Miskatonic River Valley laid the groundwork for what would eventually become *Reanimators* (2013), *The Weird Company* (2014), *Reanimatrix* (2016), *The Peaslee Papers* (2017), *The Miskatonic University Spiritualism Club* (2021), and *The Eldritch Equations* (2022). His short story collection, *The Strange Company and Others*, was released in 2019. He has edited two anthologies, one with Brian Sammons, *Legacy of the Reanimator* (2015); and *The Chromatic Court* (2019), a collection of Lovecraftian stories inspired by the King in Yellow. He is a regular member of the Lovecraft Ezine Podcast and a frequent contributor to the *New York Review of Science Fiction*.

Pete has also made a series of contributions to Wild Hunt Press, with short stories related to his Lovecraftian continuity appearing in the anthologies *Dorian Gray: Darker Shades* (2018) and *Duel of the Monsters Volume 1* (2019) &

Volume 2 (2021). *Dorian Gray vs. Reanimator* (2023) is his first big project for WHP.

Christofer Nigro is a lifelong fan of the horror, sci-fi, and fantasy genres in any given medium, and has been an avid collector and reader of comic books as long as he can remember. He has also wanted to be a writer for most of his life, and has had short stories, flash fiction, novellas, and novels published by Black Coat Press, Sirens Call Publications, Pro Se Press, Grinning Skull Press, Local Hero Press, Horrified Press, and Severed Press. His work has included extended character arcs for the Phantom of the Opera and Felifax the Tiger-Man in Volumes 8-20 of *Tales of the Shadowmen*, an annual multi-author anthology from Black Coat Press featuring the exploits of heroes & villains from classic French pulp fiction prose and cinema.

Chris is the founder, publisher, and editor-in-chief of Wild Hunt Press, through which he has published his teen werewolf horror series *Nero* (beginning with *Nero Book 1: The Beast Emerges*), and being a long-time fan of the shared universe concept, he has begun expanding the Nero Universe, along with the greater Wild Hunt Universe – a pulp hero/villain and monster universe

— in general, into a saga of separate but interconnected series.

His daikaiju universe, the DragonStorm Universe, has recently received a new lease on life courtesy of Raven Tale Publishing, who has released new editions of his kaiju horror novels *Megadrak: Beast of the Apocalypse* and *Megadrak: Tokyo Screams*.

He is now hard at work planning the re-launch of yet another shared alternate reality, a super-hero universe known as the Warp Event Universe, which will pave the way with new editions of his gritty super-hero novels *Centurion: Dark Genesis* and *Moonstalker: A Knight in Buffalo*.

Chris is likewise known for being the architect of websites such as The Godzilla Saga and The Warrenverse: The Amazing World of the Warren Comic Book Characters, which he plans to upgrade in the future. He also spent a year co-hosting Rob Wronski Jr.'s now defunct but (hopefully!) fondly remembered Television Crossover Universe podcast.

Kevin Heim was born in 1969 in Louisville, Kentucky, and was raised by Scooby-Doo cartoons, which taught him a love for crossovers. He retired from the military at age 40 and shortly thereafter moved to Salem, Massachusetts to experience the New England found in Stephen King and H. P. Lovecraft stories. Though he has very few things published to date, he has been writing fiction since he could read, which suggests he hasn't been reading for very long.

Nevertheless, he is slowly but surely building an oeuvre, with his debut published credit being a short story appearing in the 2012 *Psychopomp Hallowe'en Special* from Vietnamese Wallflowers. He has since become a fixture with Wild Hunt Press, having short stories appearing in the anthologies *Dorian Gray: Darker Shades*; *Duel of the Monsters Volume 1*; and *Boogey Knights: Dark Warriors*.

MEANDERING PATHS:
BOOK ONE

FIRST STEPS

ILLUSTRATIONS   CONCEPT ART
CREATURES   CHARACTERS

LUNGGA
CREATIVES

COVER ART   STORY ART   TITLE ART

LUNGGACREATIVES@GMAIL.COM